RUNEMASTER
SHIELD MAIDEN'S BLADE

AIRSHIP 27 PRODUCTIONS

Runemaster: Shield Maiden's Blade
© 2021 Mike Bullock

Published by Airship 27 Productions
www.airship27.com
www.airship27hangar.com

Interior illustrations© 2021 Chris Nye
Cover illustration© 2021 Steve Otis

Editor: Ron Fortier
Associate Editor: Jonathan Sweet
Marketing and Promotions Manager: Michael Vance
Production Designer: Rob Davis.

ISBN: 978-1-946183-99-6

Printed in the United States of America

10 9 8 7 6 5 4 3 2 1

RUNEMASTER
SHIELD MAIDEN'S BLADE

by Mike Bullock

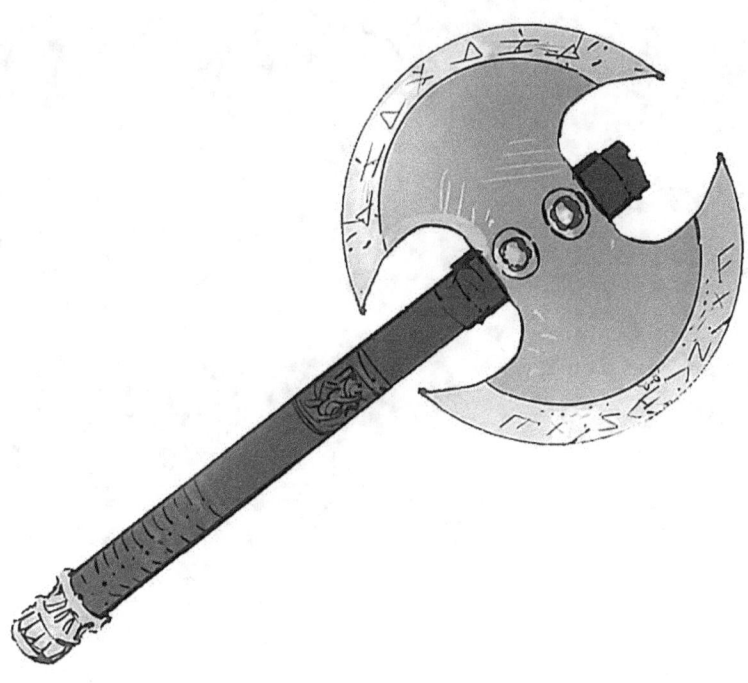

PROLOGUE: *BLOOD IN THE FROST*

The icy wind assaulted my flesh with a thousand frozen needles that slipped through my chainmail, piercing my skin everywhere at once. The animal furs draped over the plates on my shoulders did little to abate the invasion of cold. I yearned deep within to hear the crackle and feel the warmth of the fire in our Great House, but knew it was not to be on this early morning. Nine sun falls had passed since my banishment from the clan. But last night my Father, Jarl Kirwall, the Runemaster, had returned from his sojourn to the south. With him came my vindication, of this I was sure. I continued my march, pushing one foot at a time down through the thin veneer of ice that had formed over the deep snow overnight. The crunch of each step heralded my descent from the caves in the foothills of the Nir Mountains. Anticipation filled me with impatience, making each moment seem like an eternity. My heart wanted to run, but I was trudging as quickly as the deep snow would allow, drawing closer to my ancestral home with every laborious step.

Had Father been there ten days ago, events would have transpired differently. Dishonor and shame may not have been cast on me so easily. While clan chieftain, Sigurd Angivar and the council of elders governed the clan, Father, the clan Runemaster, had final say in all things pertaining to the law, judged by the gods themselves. His will that justice be done was unyielding – this was the way of all Runemasters from time immemorial as set in motion by Adon, king of the gods.

It was said Adon roamed the world, keeping an eye on us, but caring little for our troubles. No, he sought to find the heartiest warriors, those who overcame the greatest challenges, those who fought righteously to achieve glory. Legends told of the great army he was building for the final day of reckoning. To gain his attention, to have him notice us that we might not only join his army but gain a position of leadership within it was the greatest honor we could hope to achieve in this life.

Adon also abhorred treachery. The sort I'd come to know all too well of late. I'd had no other choice but to leave when Sigurd and the council pronounced me guilty of treason against my brothers. While the ignominy stung my pride, in my heart of hearts, I failed to believe this was anything other than a temporary affront. I knew that once Father returned, I would have the chance to speak my peace and prove that I was not complicit in the schemes in which I had been accused by the vile Tristan. It helped not my case that he was Sigurd's only son and had lived in my shadow since childhood. His hand of jealousy was all over this, I had but to prove it to Father now, for Sigurd would hear none of it.

This very thought kept me moving forward, climbing through the knee-deep snow, girded against the bitter needling wind that pierced my armor like no weapon ever forged by the hands of man. Kirwall was but a few hours march from the camp I'd made within the caverns and I was nearly upon her. If it were spring, the trip would be but a quarter of that time, at worst. However, the last storm had laid such a deep blanket of snow upon the land that traveling any way other than horseback was an arduous journey. Even our mighty warhorses would move far slower than normal through this.

In the moments before dawn, the light ahead from the clan's campfires gave off a warm orange glow, shining up the hill that led from the caves to our village and illuminating my icy breath as it escaped my lips. The realization of my journey's end sent new vigor through my limbs and I redoubled my pace. I would be home soon, warming myself beside the hearth, where vindication awaited me.

Father had returned last night, of that I was certain. However, I knew if I arrived before he awoke in the morning, I would surely have to cross swords with Einar Jor'Heim's warriors who stood guard every eve. Einar was our military commander, a role he inherited after Kjell Helvig, Father's best friend, who fell in battle not long ago. While my pride still stung from my unceremonious exile, I had no desire to spill the blood of a fellow clansman nor dishonor the will of the council. No, I would avoid any of my fellow warriors until I could meet with Father.

I plodded on through the tundra as the crest of the rising sun ignited a million lights upon the permafrost. The dazzling imagery never ceased to take my breath away for the briefest of moments. Many a morning my precious Lacina and I had stolen away to share the spectacle of a new day dawning. Thinking of her full lips curved into a passionate smile and the gentle touch of her delicate fingers on my skin warmed my heart, even as the bitter wind chilled my flesh. Imaging the curvaceous form of the shield-maiden, her golden curls woven into warrior braids along each side of her beautiful face before descending onto her ivory shoulders, ignited a fire within my breast – one I had increasingly felt in her presence – was this love? Desire? Fate? I knew not, but I did know full well the notion of being near her excited something within me that I could not control.

As I tramped up the hill, knowing our village was just beyond the crest, I could barely contain my elation at the thought of how good it was to be home again; to put all of this behind me, so that I could continue my training. For, soon the day would come when my Father's axe would be mine. The secret of the Runes etched into the blade would be writ upon my soul as I, Skarl Kirwall, ascended to the rank of Runemaster. Like Father before me, I was fated to replace him just as he'd replaced my grandfather. This was how it had always been. The stories of such ascensions, spoken in Old Runish, were shared with us 'round evening fires all of my life.

But first, I had to remove the dishonor from my name.

CHAPTER ONE: *THE RUIN OF KIRWALL*

Time seemed to stand still as my gaze came across the hilltop overlooking my ancestral home. My mind could not process what I saw, instead going into a momentary state of shock as the blood of my clansmen stained the virgin snow under the feet of our ancient enemies, the Yslings. It seemed as if every inch of our village was covered in blood, fire and death. Kirwall was comprised of three Great House's a dozen long houses, several out buildings designated for food preparation and storage and the central clearing. The smoking ruins of my family's Great House blocked out the rising sun and pulled my mind backward in remembrance. Not even the cacophony of steel ringing out from the seemingly endless battle could hold my faculties to this place. It was as if the sight before me was more than my mind could bear.

I had been one of them until the last full moon. Now, I stood on the outside, no longer a member of the Kirwall clan, exiled into the wilderness. I was a renegade, an outcast, a warrior without a home, betrayed by he who wanted the hand of my beloved Lacina for his own. And who was he to challenge me? Was I not the heir to the line of Kirwall Runemasters that stretched back to the days when the gods knit our world in the roots of Reimdar? I cared not if Tristan was the son of the Chieftain, he had always been my lesser in everything.

There he stood, shoulder to shoulder with the vile Yslings as they cast destruction upon my kinsmen. At first my mind could not accept what my eyes told them – why was he not attacking our ancient enemies? Why were they not laying him low, just as they were doing to the rest of our clans-men? But then the truth found purchase in my thoughts: he was a traitor to us all – this was why he cast blame at my feet – to hide his own deception! His name would now be the scourge of the Kirwall clan, forever spoken as a curse. The name I'd come to loath over the last few weeks.

Tristan Angivar.

How had I not seen it? How could I have been so blind to the spiteful machinations of one who came in second to me time and again since the earliest days of our youth? In the warrior games we played as boys, was he not always the leader of the lost? During the Tolkengaard, our rite of passage, was it not Tristan whose fingernails dug into the rock on which I stood triumphant, mere moments too late to prevent me from reaching the mighty crag first? I always looked upon his smaller frame, his down cast visage, with the sort of pity one might hold for a wounded animal. All these years, I blindly assumed he was my friend… it would seem he held me in a different regard. And that perspective had no end to the evil it might write upon our clan's destiny.

And, the way he eyed Lacina… It seemed normal to gaze upon her with awe as her beauty was without equal in the North Lands. The angelic, heart-shaped face, the deep blue waters of her shimmering eyes, the golden curls of her long silken hair that fell upon her slender, yet supple form… the blood of Queens ran through her veins and the collective beauty of her ancestors graced her appearance. That she was one of the fiercest young shield-maidens our clan had ever seen did not detract from these things, indeed it merely added to her… *majesty.*

Mayhap I was too smitten with my love to even notice how Tristan leered at her when none thought he was about. My own hubris simply took it for another triumph over him: yet one more grain of truth that I was the one, entitled from birth to lead the Kirwall clan when Father's time ended. I had mistakenly assumed Tristan was accepting of his lot in life – was his father not the Chieftain? Although, Sigurd Angivar seemed to sally back and forth between disappointment and disgust with his son. Forever standing in the shadow of one such as myself, just as his father, Sigurd had stood in the shadow of Jarl Kirwall. I'd always found it unsettling that his own father had less use for Tristan than did the rest of us. I'd once over-heard some merchants discussing it, lamenting how sad a fate it was the gods had cast upon Tristan. But, it is not the Kirwall way to accept pity, even from oneself.

Had I only seen…

I shall never forget the day when I returned from the sacred hunt, stag on the litter, ready for the slaughter. Such a magnificent beast as it was had not been brought back to the village since the summer months. Surely, I would be praised once more for my contributions to the clan. Surely, the unceasing praise of which I'd grown accustomed would pour out again at my feet as the clan gave thanks for the provision I offered, which I also took for granted.

Alas, praise was not to be my fate that day. No… 'twas the wine of betrayal that I was forced to drink…

A sudden movement in my direction woke me from my reverie. I raised my sword just in time to ward off the blow from a formidable Ysling warrior, his grey flesh pulled taught over an abundance of muscle and sinew. He was easily twelve seasons or more my elder, thick of thew and barrel-chested, he swung upon me as if he were aiming to fell a mighty oak with one blow. The force of his sword upon mine nearly rid me of my blade. But, he had not reckoned on the anger that welled within my breast, *the rage* I had kindled for the past ten days since my betrayal. No, he had not counted the cost of his assault ere he struck and for that, he would pay.

With a few whispered words in Old Runish that were old when the world was young, I cast a spell of the berserker. A simple thing taught to Runemasters at a young age, the spell turned the caster and any of shared blood within sight into living war machines. While the spell brought with it heightened speed, dexterity and strength, the aftermath of its use took a heavy toll, leaving behind a weighty exhaustion. Due to this, casting it more than once a day was ill advised. Without it now, however, none of my clan might live to see another dawn.

Our blades met with a mighty clash again and again as he tried to hew his way through my guard like one might chop through haggard wheat on harvest day. Thanks to the spell, I fended off each blow with the zeal of one freshly awakened from a long sleep. After allowing his fervent swings to fall upon my blade for several moments, I found my opening and brought my sword up, under his guard, cutting through his sword arm at the elbow. His life blood sprayed upon the snow as an agonized cry escaped his lips. A cry I silenced with my two-handed down stroke, severing head from neck in a controlled berserker's rage. The spray from his throat splattered upon my face and hair, leaving bits of his flesh tangled in my golden braids. I let out a war cry to signal his entrance into the Great House of the afterlife.

"YYYYIIIIIIAAAAHHHHHHH!"

But the mighty Ysling's death was not enough to slake my blade and forgetting my prior reverie, I charged into the fray, hacking and slashing as I went, dealing death upon our enemies as if I were sent by Thyr himself to harvest souls for his eternal graveyards in Hel.

I clashed with one red-haired warrior after another, as my blade sang the song of battle. With a deft parry here, violent thrust there, I was soon in their midst, severing limbs and cleaving skulls. Unlike my clan, where a number of ancestral bloodlines mixed and merged, providing a wide diversity of physical appearances, the Yslings were fabled to have all descended from one man, the demi-god Ysvik. His ashen grey skin, blood red hair and piercing black eyes were described in great detail in stories meant to frighten children at bedtime. Their chieftain, Viggo, enforced their age-old belief that this purity of blood gave them superiority over all others.

While most of my Kirwall brethren were taller than my foes, and I the tallest of them, the Yslings were thick-bodied, stout warriors, known for their powerfully muscled frames. More than once my blade took purchase in a thick arm or leg, pulling me off-guard slightly as I redoubled my efforts to free my steel. Had it not been for the spell, this certainly would have been my undoing. Alas, the rage heightened my reflexes, increased my balance and ignited a fire in my blood that flooded the muscles throughout my frame. Thankfully, while I endured a dozen or more nicks and superficial wounds, none were able to land a killing stroke upon me.

I chopped my way to the center of the Ysling mob, where my sword met that of one of their leaders I'd spied standing with Tristan *the traitor* only moments earlier. The grey flecks in his red beard belied his age, which was almost imperceptibly present in his less than liquid movement. However, what he lacked in youthful dexterity, he more than made up for in guile and strength. He pressed me back with his systematic assault, blocking my every attempt to end this encounter as quickly as the last. Little did I know he was driving me back into a pile of corpses: the fallen bodies of several of my clansmen.

Once my right heel struck a body behind me, I stumbled briefly, ducking down to dodge a left to right swing from his broad sword. When I was at my lowest point, he kicked a large clump of crimson snow upon my face, temporarily blinding me.

Thankfully, my Father had prepared me for such tricks, teaching me to fight blindfolded when I was but ten winters old. Anticipating the Chieftains' next move, I spun around on my left heel, bringing my blade in a wide circle that ended as it bit deep into his legs, sheering through one before lodging in the other.

With a quick motion wiping the bloody snow from my eyes I watched him fall in a heap upon the crimson snow. Wasting no time, I turned to see a slathering pack of Ysling warriors charging me, like the rabid curs they were.

But, the berserker's spell I'd cast was more than a match for any ten Yslings! My sword wove a web of silver and red death about me, maiming or killing all those I encountered for what seemed an eternity. I'm not sure when during the battle I came to see there were nothing but Yslings left, but the realization that all of my clansmen had fallen at their hands brought me to pause for the briefest of moments… moments I would regret.

The blow that struck the back of my head would have crushed the skull of a lesser man. As it was, it split my helm and sent me tumbling into darkness.

+++

The icy fog blurred my vision, but just ahead I could see her, dancing in the Nir-frost, the blue silken dress clinging seductively to every curve of her sumptuous form. Her ample bosom rose and fell with the passionate breath of life she exuded to all within her presence. The long curls of her blond hair bounced playfully with her every movement, as the twin braids, pulled from her forehead around to her shoulders tried in vain to contain them before releasing them at the base of her skull to dance about her shoulders. While her supple shape seemed blurred by the fog, her eyes pierced the mists like the fire of pure sapphires, captivating my every thought. I reached out for her, almost involuntarily, and then the sharp blackness struck my mind like a thousand pick-hammers.

Tensing my muscles, I was able to ward off the onslaught of pain long enough to call out to her.

"La—Lacina-"

And then the blackness overwhelmed her, sweeping her from my vision and replacing her form with icy nails of stabbing pain that throbbed with every surge of wind. I set my mind to fight through to her, for nothing would stand between my beloved and me, but then his voice shattered the fog like a war hammer through the surface of a frozen pond.

"Skarl!"

I knew this voice. It was nearly as familiar as mine own. It brought with it more reverie, of the days of youth, when warrior games and mischief filled the hours between my lessons.

"SKARL!"

The demanding tone of the voice was equally familiar. I felt my lips tighten in an involuntary smirk, at once annoyed and soothed by the voice I knew so well.

"Skarl! *Wake. Up!*"

I opened mine eyes and saw the face of Runolf before me. My best friend since birth. Oddly, he was not sufficiently dressed for a day of battle, barely wearing more than his night clothing and hauberk. I knew at once where I was. "Surely I must be in The Grand Hall of the Gods now, as all mighty Kirwalls have gone to dine with Red Thorr!"

"'Grand Hall of the Gods?' Ha! Seems that blow scrambled your brain like duck eggs!" blurted Runolf, holding my split helmet in one hand. "No, Skarl. You're very much alive, but only thanks to that blasted thick skull of yours. The Yslings have gone. Lucky for you they took you for dead. And why not, a blow that splits a helmet splits a skull!"

"Alive? By Skladi's frost if I do yet draw breath. And how is it you are still here on Njordica, my friend? What fate held you back from the Grand Afterlife?"

"Those blasted Yslings swarmed upon me, knowing they could not best a man such as me single-handed. After slaying nigh a dozen of them, I slipped upon the entrails of one of their warchiefs and fell into the snow. The pile of their dead washed over me, burying me in the stench of Ysling death. While I could see everything that transpired, I was unable to remove myself from the bodies. That is, until after they left and Yulmir, my ever-faithful steed," Runolf motioned to the chestnut brown warhorse milling about the ruins, "pulled me from their cursed carcasses."

"But, what of the others? Ulf? Ingvar? Jotus? What of... Father?" I asked the questions, but already knew the answers as I'd seen the Runemaster's sacred axe lying in the ruins outside our Great House.

Runolf looked upon the ground before laying his hand on my bicep. "Aye, they are indeed dining in the Grand Hall of the Gods this very moment, my friend."

"And what of Lacina? I saw her—dancing in the Nir-Frost!"

"A vision mayhap, a fever dream induced by the blow to your skull," Runolf replied, with lowered tone and downcast eyes. "The Yslings took her, claiming she is to be sacrificed to their god, Ysfang, the World Serpent... I'm sorry my friend. I tried to save her but they overwhelmed us so suddenly."

"But, where was Jor'Heim and his riders? How could Kirwall have fallen so easily with the mightiest warriors in all of Njordica to defend her?"

"Treachery..." hissed Runolf, spitting upon the ground after he spoke the word, as if to expel the very taste of it from his mouth.

"What do you mean...?" I inquired forcefully, grabbing my friend's hauberk and nearly lifting his shorter, yet equally powerful frame from his footprints. He merely stared back with that look I'd seen countless times before. Runolf and I knew each other well; we often finished each other's sentences, conveying more in shared glances and facial expressions than mere words ever could.

"*Tristan!*" I blurted, as the realization of this all came to me.

"Yes, Skarl. Tristan," Runolf replied with a sneer curling his upper lip in disgust. "That weasel convinced the council you were making deals with the Yslings to hand over our lands, all the while he was the one double-dealing."

"But... how-?" I muttered trying to force my mind to process all that had happened.

"After you were banished, he made advances on Lacina, but she rebuked him. I'd wager he had some deal with the Yslings to set him up as the new leader of Kirwall. He fancied Lacina as his bride, but she would have none of it. I noticed how his demeanor toward her changed just yesterday, like that of a lover spurned, but I merely took joy in the fact that he could not win her over as easily as he had the council. Oh, would I have only discerned the true meaning of his change of heart.

"Right before supper last night, he stormed into your Father's Great House, rousing all of Kirwall, decrying an invasion by the Yslings through the Nir Valley Pass. Jor'Heim and his men rode out to repel the invasion, alas they never returned..."

"But... all this..." I waved my arms outward to take in the smoldering ruins of the Long Houses and Great Houses of Kirwall, and the masses of broken bodies that had been its people. "How could they?"

"The Yslings rode in at sunrise, with helms of Jor'Heim's riders 'pon their heads. In the frost light, we thought our warriors were returning. By the time we realized the truth, they were among us... It seems not only had Tristan betrayed you, but his own flesh and blood – I watched as he murdered Sigurd then welcomed the enemy into our midst. The last I saw of him, he was riding off side-by-side with the Ysling Warchief with Lacina as his prize..."

"And what of you, my friend?" I asked, still piecing the bloody puzzle together in my mind.

"The cries of our women and children roused me to combat. I emerged from my Long House, Kira by my side, and nary a stitch of clothing on. I had but a moment to don my hauberk and grab my axe and sword before they were at my very door…"

Runolf's eyes misted over suddenly, as the emotion of his experience fell upon him for the first time. The curtain of battle lust parted and the impact of his losses struck him full upon the shoulders. "But… K-k-Kira…"

"And, N-Nikolas… m-my son… they… they…" and Runolf collapsed to his knees, as if the weight of his memories were more than he could bear, driving his thick frame into the ground as his shoulders convulsed while he fought back sobs.

I lay my hand on his head, as if to bear his loss with him. But, try as I might, I could not pull my gaze from the ruins of our Great House, the largest house in all of Kirwall. The flames consumed what was left of her mighty walls, devouring the memories of all the glorious tales told within her down through the ages. From my Grandfather, to his, and so on back hundreds of years to the first Kirwall who built her with his own hands.

The flames danced almost hypnotically, reflecting off a shining surface just outside the door to the main hall: my Father's sacred axe. The light shimmered over the runes forged into the double-edged blade, calling out to me. At first, I was only vaguely aware of the axe and its siren call. But the longer I stared into the runes, the longer it seemed, they stared back into my soul, the voices of my ancestors chanting one word, over and over, with an unrelenting rhythm that would not be denied. It drummed within my mind, pounded in my heart, thumped through my veins. The chant was undeniably relentless.

REVENGE.

As the word thundered into my very soul, a flicker of hope burned within my heart. Mayhap Lacina yet still drew breath. Perhaps it was not too late to save her… this thought steeled my resolve.

There was but one path the Yslings could have taken, back to the Nir Valley Pass, the only way an army so large could traverse the Nir Mountains. The spider's web of caves that riddled the ancient crags would allow the passage of a handful of men, but no army could travel through them with any sort of speed. Runolf and I had exhausted many a youthful afternoon after our fighting lessons with Kjell, Father's best friend and one of the clan's mightiest warriors, exploring those caverns. We had spent hour after hour combing the caves for hidden treasures and imagined secrets till he and I alone knew them far better than any of our clansmen. But, despite all our time in them, even Runolf and I did not know whither they all wound.

Certainly, no Ysling could navigate their stygian depths with any degree of certainty. No, they would take the Pass, for through the caverns lay the end of an army. Yes, the pass it was.

With the thought of avenging the Clan Kirwall beating on the drum of my heart, and the hope of saving my beloved Lacina igniting a flame within my breast I scarcely realized I had left my friend's side striding purposefully toward the remains of my home. Runolf's eyes followed my footsteps, knowing my thoughts faster than I.

"Let me gather my armor and we'll ride them down like the dogs they are!" he snarled.

His words seemed to come to me from some barely remembered dream. For, my focus was locked upon the sacred axe lying in the crimson frost. My hands closed upon its haft, lifting it from the pile of bodies that surrounded it. And, that's when mine eyes fell upon him fully for the first time. My dear Father, split open from throat to groin, undoubtedly by an Ysling's sword. Judging from the dozens of dead Yslings around him, my Father had taken account of our enemy before he fell. They had paid a heavy price to purchase his life with their swords. Oddly, I found myself fixating on the fact that he was wearing little more than his sleep gown. The thought that a mighty warrior such as he would ride into the courtyard of the Grand Hall of the Gods adorned not in his finest armor, but a cotton robe brought a mist to mine eyes.

His blank gaze stared on into eternity, as if his now lifeless body were trying to pierce the veil of the afterlife itself, to see where my Father's soul had gone. A single tear ran through the dried blood on my face. But, tears were not the way of the Kirwall warriors, and the first died a lonely death upon the frozen ground at my Father's side.

"We shall avenge them all, my brother!" Runolf decried, now suited for battle in chainmail woven by his lost bride. A steel helmet, engraved with the skeletal wings of a Nir Hawk upon each side. "Come, Skarl! your Father's horse – and vengeance —awaits!"

I lifted the axe of my Father and his father before him, captivated by it as I had been since I first was old enough to understand what it meant to wield a weapon such as this. Around the edges of the blade were cast sacred runes in Old Runish, the dead dialect known only to the Runemasters. Those runes could unlock powers most mortals could not withstand, as evidenced by the piles of Ysling bodies surrounding my Father's unarmored form.

"No, Runolf," I replied in a cold tone. "We take to the caves. Remember the path of the ice worm? We shall travel through the dark passages and meet them on the far side, and there... there we shall have our revenge."

CHAPTER TWO: *BREATH OF THE WORM*

The warmth of the caves did little to melt the chill from my heart. No matter what sort of blizzard assaulted the Nir Mountains, these caverns were always a constant temperature, warm in comparison. Runolf and I had entered through an opening south of the Nir Valley Pass and left our horses behind to fend for themselves. Both were hearty animals, but with nothing left of Kirwall, I doubted their ability to survive for long. Hopefully their instincts would lead them south to the Angar Clan, where they would be welcomed as the powerful steeds they were.

We moved quickly through the rocky outcroppings, dodging both stalactite and stalagmite with the dexterity born of a childhood spent exploring these caves. The luminescent moss that grew upon the cavern ceiling cast a comforting green glow upon our path. While we knew the Ysling warriors were at least a few hours ahead of us when we first left Kirwall, we counted on our ability to make time through the caverns to head them off at the other side of the pass. A choke point existed, roughly halfway through the exit from the Nir Valley, where the Yslings would be forced to travel two abreast. Sheer rock on either side went up to the height of five tall men. If we could make it to the other side of the choke point before the Yslings, Runolf and I could certainly slay them two by two until no Ysling remained.

The breakneck pace was beginning to take its toll on our bodies, however, as neither of us had eaten since the night before. The after-effects of the berserker spell weighed down my limbs, but my will overcame as best I could. My estimation put us at mid-day now and while we were trained to go several sun rises without food, consuming nothing more than melted snow, a day such as today was something we'd never anticipated.

Runolf wouldn't allow a selfish complaint to escape his lips, but I could see the fatigue in his eyes. We'd not let up from our harried pursuit since leaving Kirwall two hours after dawn. Knowing we had no time to waste, but could nary afford to overtake the Yslings in a state of exhaustion, I decided it was best to seek refreshment.

"Runolf, remember the pool up ahead? I say we stop for a moment, fill our skins with fresh water, douse our thirst and then continue."

"Agreed," Runolf replied with a devilish gleam in his eye. "Wouldn't want you getting run through due to a parched throat; you utter enough excuses already."

A brief smile curled the left side of my mouth as we continued to climb and duck our way through the caverns. As children, we'd come to this pool and sat upon its edges, regaling each other with fabricated tales of gods and giants, warriors and women. My mind smiled at the remembrances and wondered why we'd stop coming here so long ago. It was a place of solace for us, a place where we were free from the shackles of our lives, free to dream and become the mighty warriors we had been told about around the village fires since we were old enough to listen.

As we crawled through a particularly tight section of the caverns, forced to move on our hands and knees, we could hear the reverberation of water dripping from the ceiling into the pool ahead. Within moments we were through the crawl space and into the wider cavern.

It was just as we remembered; seeming almost magical as the greenish glow from the moss reflected off the tranquil water and sent shimmering fingers of light dancing across the walls of the cave. It had seemed a far larger space in our youth, but it did allow us to stand upright and stretch our frames for the first time in nearly an hour.

"It seems like forever... and yesterday..." Runolf mused, looking into the deep waters of the pool as if he were staring back through time. He dipped his empty skin into the waters, dispersing his reverie as the vessel broke the water's surface, sending ripples across the pool.

"Has it really been five winters since we were here last?" I asked, more to myself than Runolf. Once we'd passed the Tolkengaard, we no longer had the free time of children to frolic in the caverns. We'd set aside our youthful dalliances for the way of the warrior.

Runolf pulled a hunk of bread from his pack, tore it two and handed half to me. "We should eat..."

Sinking my teeth into the doughy bundle, I stared into the water, now finding myself lost in the placid shimmer. As we ate, my mind traveled back to a time when I had convinced Runolf the stalactites above were actually the roots of the very mountains, reaching downward to dig into the beating heart of our world. We imagined them growing deeper and deeper, through rock, water, earth and -

From the corner of my eye, I swore I'd seen one of the stalactites move. At the realization, the hackles on the back of my neck stood erect and a tingle shot down my spine. Involuntarily, I gripped the haft of Father's weapon as it hung upon my belt. My ears strained to listen, as if to hear the very sound of the mountains reaching down into the world, but I heard nothing.

Then—something.

It was less a noise at first as it was a feeling of the air pressure change, felt almost imperceptibly on my ear drums. We had been trained long ago to notice these things, in order to avoid anyone attempting to sneak upon us in the darkness. But this, this felt larger, more powerful than any Ysling. I turned and looked at Runolf, questioning with my eyes to see if he had noticed the same sensation.

And then it was upon us!

+++

It is truly strange what thoughts assail the mind in moments of stress. I've often wondered if these cognitive detours are the mind's way of warding off fear and anxiety, as if focusing too much on one's own impending doom might be more than any one heart could bear? Those of our clan seldom, if ever, felt fear or anxiety. But even so, these occurrences still took my thoughts captive, leading them on a tangent of sorts from current events, even if only for the briefest of instances.

I know not how young I was when Father first began my training to replace him as Runemaster. All I can recall is that it was always this way. Half-remembered moments mixed with vivid memories as I looked back on my life thus far. While these recollections flew through my mind like an angry storm wind on a cold morning, I felt the need to include them here to help you further understand the calling placed upon my life.

Our Clan was led by a trinity of men, the Chieftain, the Seer and the Runemaster. This was the way it had always been, back through the ages.

Sigurd Angivar, whose body now lay in the burning ruins of a village, betrayed by his own son Tristan, was responsible for day to day tasks of governance and provision.

The Seer, whose whereabouts I was unable to discern, was a divine emissary, sent long ago to educate and counsel us in the will of the gods. No one knew, not even Father, when he was born and many considered him immortal. Although more often than not he spoke in vague riddles and fever dreams from the smoke of the sage and hycosum plants used in his rituals of spiritual communication, his words were not to be disregarded lightly.

The administration of justice and military control was left to the Runemaster. It was also up to him to interpret the Seer's visions and prophecies. With a variety of spells, from the simple berserker and healing spells

AND THEN IT WAS UPON US.

to the more advanced *forevision*, which gave the Runemaster a limited ability to see the future of a battle and *deadspeak*, which allowed him to glean information from those who recently died in battle, the range of spells grew as the Runemaster matured. Wisdom and maturity also imbued the Runemaster with an innate ability to ferret out dishonesty, an attribute Father employed more than once during my childhood on the few occasions I tried to lie my way out of whatever trouble I'd gotten into.

Use of these spells required at least a basic knowledge of Old Runish, for the simpler ones, and a mastery of it for the more advanced ones. Unfortunately, my training was not yet complete nor was my advanced understanding of the Runic words. Without Father to complete my training, I wondered whither I might turn to further my knowledge and wisdom. Unfortunately, we'd left in such haste I'd forgotten to take the satchel of runes from Father's possessions. Perhaps they would escape the fire and still be there, waiting for my return. If that day ever came...

+++

"YYYAAAAAARRRR!"

Runolf's battle cry shattered my momentary reverie, barely escaping his lips before the slimy tendril wrapped about him and lifted him bodily from the floor of the cave. I cursed under my breath as the realization struck me, I wasn't looking at a stalactite reflected in the pool, but this monster's tendril as it came down from the ceiling to crush the life from my friend.

In surprising him, the thing had managed to pin Runolf's sword arm to his side. It had lifted him nearly over my head in but an instant. Without thinking, I swung my father's axe at the slimy tendril and cut deep into its unholy flesh. Black ichor sprayed out from the wound, hitting me full in the face and temporarily blinding me. However, the impact of the blade must have severed some muscle tissue as the thing dropped Runolf to the cavern floor. He landed upon a broken stalagmite with a sickening thud that possibly meant broken ribs, if nothing else. Oddly, the creature made no sound whatsoever. Aside from Runolf's landing and initial surprise, the entire scene would have played out in utter silence.

As I dragged my left backhand across my eyes to wipe away the slime, another tendril shot in from the darkness, aiming to rip me from the ground as the last had done to Runolf. I batted the tip of the thing aside with the flat of my axe as a third and then a fourth shot in. The axe chopped away at tendril after tendril, until I was becoming overwhelmed. I had to find the thing's body if Runolf and I were to emerge victorious, but the stygian blackness hid the creature's form from our sight. My imagination went wild momentarily, trying to conjure an image of what this beast must look like —some long-lost horror from the age before men, risen from the depths of the world to once again assert its superiority. We had always heard tales of forgotten beasts inhabiting these caverns, but grew to believe they were merely told to scare us. The thrill of challenging such creatures in our youth drove us on, but never once had we encountered one of these legends; until now. The idea that there might be more than one of them lying in wait chilled my blood. I knew then that we needed to end this quickly. And, that's when the idea struck me.

As the next tendril shot in, I raised my arms straight up and allowed it to wrap around my torso. The creature lifted me from the ground and drew me back into the blackness of the side cavern from whence it came. The thought that the thing might dash my skull upon the rocks occurred to me briefly, but thankfully I had angered it so with my defense that it sought to devour me instantly. As it pulled me into the darkness, I spotted a reflection upon a singular, blood red eye the size of a warrior's shield, shaped like that of a serpent. It was then I caught a glimpse of the thing, a long cylindrical, ice white body—like that of a massive, frozen worm— with nigh a dozen tendrils protruding from its body just behind the bloody eye. So, this is what the fabled ice worm looked like—it appeared to share very little in common with the descriptions told to us by wanderers who came to Kirwall. Most likely as none had encountered one and lived to tell about it. Instead of gasping at the horror of the putrid ice worm, which was nearly four times longer than I was tall, I girded my thoughts, knowing I now had a target that seemed far more vulnerable than the slimy, prehensile tendrils that sought to crush me in their coils.

Suddenly, a silver streak shot past me on the right, and extinguished the light of the great eye! And then, the thing released me as the tendrils thrashed about frantically before withdrawing deeper into the impenetrable darkness. I dropped to the cavern floor, able to avoid landing awkwardly since my arms remained free throughout the ordeal. As I lifted my axe and prepared to renew the battle, I saw the other tendrils withdraw, one by one, disappearing into the depths of the alcove until only Runolf and I remained in the cavern of the pool.

Once I assured myself of the thing's departure, I returned to Runolf, to check on his condition. He sat there by the side of the pool, grinning like a fool.

"It seems strange creatures have taken up residence since last we frolicked here, my good Runolf," I declared. "I wonder whence it slithered..."

"To remove my long knife from its eye, most likely."

"Ha ha ha!" an involuntary belly laugh escaped my lips, as the thought of the beast writhing in agony brought mirth to my heart.

"Do you remember the tales of the ice worm, Runolf? Told to us by travelers when we were just boys? All these years I thought them mere fantasy, embellished by men seeking to frighten young boys."

"Aye, seems they are more than legend after all."

"Come, let's move on before the beast returns for more. Unless, that is, you wish to reclaim your long knife?"

"Yahh —let the worm choke on it."

And with that, we filled our water skins, cleaned the creature's blood from our flesh, slaked our thirst and moved on through the caves toward the Nir Pass and my beloved Lacina.

+++

"Parry!"

All together there were twelve of us, some fiercely participating, some half-heartedly doing so. But, we were all to learn the way of the axe, war hammer and sword as every Kirwall child before us had. Fighting was as much a way of life as breathing. And, the only way to gain entrance to the fabled halls of the afterlife was to die honorably, which for most, meant falling in battle. If one didn't know how to fight, then dying defenselessly in a fight would lack that honor, casting our next life into an abyss of nothingness. This existence had too much pain, too much suffering for anyone to simply hope that was all there was and upon the moment of death for everything to simply end.

WHACK!

Runolf's wooden practice sword caught me full upon the side of the head, knocking me from my reverie —and my feet! We were both but ten winters old, as were all the young ones gathered in this battle practice, yet he and I showed promise above and beyond the other children. Our fathers had spent long hours teaching us the finer points of single combat, which we then refined through pretend battles with all sorts of foes, both human and beast. In fact, most of our spare time was spent dreaming up some imaginary conflict that required our swords to win the day.

Cl-CLACK! CLACK!

Regaining my composure, I closed on Runolf in a series of calculated swings, meant to push his wooden blade to the left, before feinting that way and striking to his right.

WHUMP!

The tip of my blade caught him in the right shoulder, as he had over-extended to defend his left. The resulting action found him down on his backside, sword in no position to prevent a killing blow.

"Curse you Skarl Kirwall!" Runolf yelled, half in frustration, half in playful taunt.

Lowering my sword, I laughed at my friend, as he sought to get back to his feet before our instructor could chastise him for his overextension that led to my victory. It was then, I learned another valuable lesson.

WHACK!

The blow hit me in the back of the head, sending me full into Runolf's downed form.

"Ha! It would seem even the mighty Skarl Kirwall has a weakness: his own ego!" While this was not the first time this voice entered my mind, it was the first time I truly *heard* it. Turning quickly, I saw her, standing over us laughing, playfully, with a look of triumph that seemed majestic on that face, one I could describe as nothing short of mesmerizingly beautiful. Looking back, it was in this moment I first became aware of my feelings for her. Several other girls stood beside her, laughing at us playfully.

"Don't bother getting up; you're hardly the first warriors to fall under the blade of Kirwall's vaunted shield-maidens!" Had anyone else mocked me thusly, I'd have experienced anger welling up from within, but for some reason I found myself enjoying the attention this shield-maiden to be was paying us.

"Lacina! That wasn't fair!" Runolf blurted out, instantly wishing he could take back those hastily spewed words.

"The only truth in battle, young Runolf," our instructor's voice bellowed for all to hear, "is that nothing is fair. Never, ever turn your back on anyone in a fight until you are positive no opponents remain breathing."

"Are we to fight girls, then?" Runolf's insistence on making matters worse continued to assert itself.

"How dare you!" fire lit from Lacina's eyes as she raised her wooden sword and verbally retaliated at the implied insult of Runolf's words.

Regaining my feet, I stepped aside so the two could face one another. Runolf, clearly not realizing how deep he was digging his own hole, brushed the snow from his pants while only half-facing her, as if she was unworthy of his full attention.

Giving her a slight nod, the instructor motioned for the rest of us to step back, forming a circle around the two of them. Before Runolf was fully aware of what was happening, she was on him with a fury our group of budding warriors had never before seen.

"Take it back!" Lacina yelled as she swatted him in the backside with the flat of her sword, before bringing it back around to in a stroke aimed at his head.

Runolf suddenly realized just what he'd gotten himself into. At our age shield maidens usually trained with other girls and male warriors with other boys, but soon the gender barriers would fall, since shield maidens were expected to fight anyone and everyone in a real battle. It wasn't unheard of for children of our age to mix in mock battles, but the winner was usually regaled for many moons after the battle and the loser more often than not mocked for their failure – particularly if it was a male defeated by a shield maiden to be.

As her back stroke closed on his head, Runolf raised his sword just in time to block the incoming swing. Employing a trick Father had once shown us, Runolf's left hand shot out and grabbed Lacina by the left shoulder and spun around – his impetus meant to pull her off balance due to the ferocity of her blow. However, I would later learn Lacina had seen me employ this trick on others – including Runolf – more than once and was prepared for it.

CRACK!

Bringing her sword backward faster than Runolf could react; the edge of the wooden blade contacted the bony part of his left wrist eliciting a yelp of pain from my friend and loss of grip on her shoulder.

The two circled one another now, Runolf fully engaged and no longer seeming to underestimate his opponent. They exchanged blows for several minutes, striking, parrying, swinging, countering back and forth, with neither seeming to gain the upper-hand. As I watched, my appreciation for Lacina grew even more. She was clearly faster and more agile than Runolf, which seemed to even the odds as he outweighed – and outmuscled her considerably.

Just as it seemed the two might fight on into the evening, the familiar, welcome chime of the dinner bell sounded, summoning us all to the Great House for a feast.

"I almost had her," Runolf muttered, trying to cover his wounded pride, as we raced to the Great House.

"I know..." my reply hardly rang true as I found myself almost ignoring my friend and hoping beyond hope Lacina would sit near us during the feast.

+++

Sunlight, reflected off the frost, shone into the caves from an opening in the distance. It was there we knew we would make our stand. We redoubled our pace to reach the opening, as concern gripped us that our dalliance with the ice worm had allowed the Yslings time to clear the pass. If such was true, our plan would certainly be undone.

Once our eyes adjusted to the blinding glare from the Nir Frost, we noted no footsteps marred the virgin snow.

We were in time!

As we made for the opening an almost imperceptible sound of metal on metal came to our ears. That noise most assuredly came from the presence of men.

The Yslings were near!

We peered cautiously from our cover within the cavern, noting the distance between the opening and the choke point. The caverns opened upon a ledge, a sword's length from the valley floor. The Nir path was not far from the lip of the ledge, but at an angle that prevented anyone beyond the choke point from having a clear view of the opening itself. We judged the distance from our position to the one we would need to take to carry out our assault, realizing we could cover the distance in a few broad strides.

I nodded to Runolf and tightened my grip upon my Father's axe, as the blood left my knuckles and my fingers dug into the leather straps wound round its steel sheathed haft. Runolf's eyes burned with an intensity born in his craving for vengeance as his face constricted with anger.

"They will pay a heavy price for the purchase of my wife and son…" Runolf snarled.

Nodding in affirmation, my mind swam with visions of Lacina, her beautiful face marred by fear and pain. This image sent my heart racing and my ears rushing as blood seemed to boil in my veins. The Yslings would certainly give account for their actions this day and I vowed to not take respite until every one of their putrid kind lay dead on the valley floor.

Tightening my grip on the axe, I started forward as the Spell of the Berserker began to escape my lips. I knew casting twice in one day would take a very heavy toll upon me, but I fully intended to have no enemies left after this encounter.

However, my casting was interrupted by Runolf's hand, clamping down upon my shoulder, pulling me back into the cave. Puzzled as to why my friend would stop me, I turned, askance, towards him.

And that's when I saw it.

+++

Twas not Runolf's calloused hand upon my shoulder, but a thick, ichor stained tendril. The ice worm had returned, seeking a reckoning with us. Before I could fully grasp the situation, another tendril shot past from left to right and slammed Runolf into the cavern wall with such violence the light in his eyes dimmed as he sunk to the floor. The sight of my friend's limp form amplified the rushing in my ears and fired a staccato drum beat through my veins. My vision ran red as I lifted the axe on high, severed the tendril that had hold of me and charged the monster, fully prepared to slaughter it or die in the attempt.

When aided with the Berserker spell, rage was an ally that fueled our battle skills. However, anger alone merely led to poor decisions, as I was soon to discover. The ice worm waited for me to close to almost within striking range and then it brought several tendrils in from behind and wrapped around me like the tree serpents I'd heard of in the steaming jungles far to the south. As I tried in vain to free my axe, another tendril ripped it from my grip and tossed it aside.

In the ensuing melee, the worm spun me around in many directions, allowing me brief glimpses of the valley pass. My subconscious mind half registered the sight of the Yslings, moving through the choke point unencumbered, while I was otherwise occupied with this icy horror of the underworld.

The beast drew me in, close to its maw once again. The red eye that had gone dim in our last encounter was partially obscured by dried, crusty ichor that oozed from a wound just above it —presumably where Runolf's long knife had struck. Of the knife, there was no sign; the creature had clearly pulled it loose and discarded it somewhere deep in the tunnels.

It was then I noticed the toothy maw, circular in shape, with several rows of needle-sharp teeth ringing the inside. That the creature meant to devour me, I have no doubt. The very idea of losing my life in this cave, to this abomination, while my precious Lacina was so close drove me to the point of frenetic action such as I'd never experienced before. Remembering my half-cast spell, I wished I'd been able to finish the incantation as the thing sought to crush the life from me before feeding upon my carcass. With a muted battle cry, I swung my right fist with all my remaining strength straight into the oozing wound above the eye. My hand thrust nearly to the elbow inside the beast. Without a moment's hesitation, I opened my fist and reached downward, grabbing the back of the eye. I sunk my fingers into the eye with all the might I could bring to bear and then pulled my arm back out of the worm's head, bringing with it the back of the eyeball itself in a mass of black blood and torn flesh.

The silent roar from the creature will haunt my dreams for the rest of my days. In its anguished spasms, it tossed me backward, toward the opening of the cave. The last thing I recall before my head struck the cavern floor was a brief glimpse of my lovely Lacina, marching past the opening in chains, pulled along by a leash around her neck.

Holding the leash was none other than Tristan Angivar.

CHAPTER THREE: *THE HUNT*

How long I lay unconscious is still unclear. The tone of sunlight outside the cave seemed to indicate it was still roughly the same time of day. However, a light dusting of snow covered the Yslings footprints on the valley floor. As I regained my senses, my first thought was of Runolf. I went immediately to my friend, hoping he was but unconscious as well. However, his eyes were open, staring after his soul which had journeyed on to Valhalla. My right fist clenched subconsciously, still holding a chunk of the worm flesh, as anger ground my teeth together and snarled across my lips. For how many crimes must Tristan pay?

I ran my fingers down Runolf's face to close his eyelids. Oddly, his face carried a serenity at this moment I'd never seen in him before. Since I had not the means to create a funeral pyre for my friend, I vowed to return once Lacina was safe and he was avenged. It almost seemed just to leave him here, in this cave, where we had spent so much of our youth enjoying life. I propped his sword in his hand and lay the nicked steel across his chest so that any who might happen upon him would know he was a true warrior.

I cast about for several moments, searching for my Father's axe. After what seemed an eternity, I spotted the rune covered blade protruding from a rocky outcropping on the far side of the cavern. Once I had retrieved the weapon, I wiped the worm flesh over the runes, allowing the creatures lifeblood to fill the engravings. I whispered a half-remembered incantation under my breath that I'd heard my Father utter at the end of each battle and watched in awe as the runes glowed blood red for the briefest of instants.

Setting the chunk of the beast's eye in Runolf's hand, I closed his fingers over it in one final gesture.

"Enjoy the feast, old friend."

I poured water down the axe blade and then into my palm to wash away the filth. Sheathing the weapon, I lifted Runolf's water skin from around his shoulders and the pack from his back. And with that, I turned and exited the caverns into the Nir Valley Pass.

+++

Kneeling beside the frozen tracks of the Yslings, I determined I'd lain unconscious in the caves for one day. The top layer of boot print at my fingertips had a hair thin sheet of ice upon it, as happens each night when the temperatures plummet to life threatening levels. A light dusting of morning snow was upon each footprint as well, some blown in, some fallen from the sky. Had I been asleep longer than one day, wind, snow and ice would have buried the tracks, yet these were only partially obscured. While there was some solace to be had in knowing I still drew breath, and with that knowledge came hope of freeing Lacina and avenging my clan, the thought I had not only failed to take advantage of the choke point, but lost an entire day's travel vexed me greatly. And, the loss of Runolf...

Without paying heed to the growl of my empty stomach, I took off at a run, determined to gain as much ground upon my prey as possible while the sun was still shining down from on high. Based on its location in the sky, I guessed it to be early afternoon, which gave me only a few hours. I had plenty of water and could satiate my hunger once I was beyond the pass and into the Valley of Glass that lay a half day's walk ahead. Just below the ice at the center of the Valley was a stream that contained sea life. Pulling a warm fish from the frozen water would certainly rid me of hunger. There was a small bit of bread left from Runolf's pack, but we'd both planned to catch game or fish to supplement our meals.

As I jogged along in the packed down snow of my quarry's path they'd blazed yesterday, I tried to gauge the number of Yslings in this war party. If memory served, they seldom ventured across the Sea of Ashgul with less than two hundred warriors. Surely more than a hundred had fallen at Kirwall, and still more to the blades of Jor'Heim's riders ere they descended upon my home. Knowing I must further reduce the odds against me, if I were to have any hope of saving Lacina, I racked my brain for a solution as I jogged on.

After what seemed about an hour or more, the icy air began stabbing into my lungs, a sure sign I had run as far as I could without rest. I slowed to a walk, still contemplating just how I would increase my chances of taking out all the Yslings. As I paced forward, the sun shone briefly through the clouds and cast a shadow down from an outcropping that extended over the pass. The sight of the overhead ice pier brought with it divine inspiration. With that came a renewed vigor as I took off at a fast jog once more. Beyond the Valley of Glass was another, far shorter pass that opened up to the Bay of Abiathar. It was there the Yslings had certainly grounded their longboats. If they made it to the boats, all hope might indeed be lost. But, if I could reach that pass before them, there was an ice bridge I might drop upon them, crushing a great many of the fiends and sowing chaos in their ranks. That would certainly afford me the advantage of surprise necessary to free Lacina and get her to safety before I could carry out my sworn vengeance.

I ran on as the sun began its daily descent into the sea. Once I realized nightfall was rapidly approaching, I spurred my legs to carry me at greater speed in the hopes of catching my prey sooner, rather than later.

Knowing the Yslings were hard pressed to move faster than a slow, steady march, I prayed I might catch a glimpse of them soon, as my hurried gait over the last several hours had certainly allowed me to gain ground. As the pass rose over a crest, I thought I saw a shimmering light ahead, the quality of which did not match that of light reflected from ice or snow. Surely, it was the Ysling war party.

I slowed to a fast walk once more, allowing my lungs to rest and draw deep, rejuvenating breaths. At first, my air came in ragged gasps as I realized I'd pushed myself a bit too hard, but after a moment or so, I was breathing normally once more. It was then I heard the sound of another living thing drawing breath behind me.

While I pursued the Yslings, apparently something far more fearsome was pursuing me.

"Grraaarrr-" It was a deep throated growl, the likes of which froze the blood of women and children. Legends and myths of fabled wolf men sprang to mind as my imagination raced ahead of reality; trying to discern what was behind me before I could ascertain what it was with my own eyes. And, then I heard it draw a deep breath and leap toward me.

+++

Spinning on my heel, I was able to duck the lunge of the massive, white and grey ice wolf, that hurtled over my head with enough force to assure me had I not turned, I'd now be pinned to the ground by its nightmarish bulk. The creature landed on its massive, mottled paws and turned back toward me with a dexterity that belied its size. A second snarl escaped the beast's black lips as they curled back on a row of blood-stained teeth book-ended by two long knife-sized incisors that hung down from its upper jaw. The fur around the frightening maw was crusted with the lifeblood of its last kill. Were I a lesser man, surely I would have fled in panic at the sheer sight of the hell hound. From tongue to tail it was a distance nearly twice my height. The fact the canine surely weighed four or five times what I did was not lost on me, either. I had seen ice wolves before, and even hunted a few, but never had I laid eyes on one as formidable as this rogue male. Then, as if to make certain it had my attention, the massive beast roared so loudly I felt my skeleton shake beneath my flesh.

"RAAAAAAAARRRR!"

I hurriedly pulled my father's axe from my belt and prepared to strike, but before I could have it at the ready, the wolf lunged for me once again. The second assault caused me to dive to the side, narrowly avoiding the dagger like claws on the monster's front paws that would have surely torn my flesh open. Before I could recover, it was upon me, crushing the breath from my lungs as its incredible weight pressed my body into the snow. The fetid stench of its breath, ripe with the rotten flesh of its last meal still dangling between its sinister fangs, assailed me and nearly choked the air from my nostrils.

I felt the things claws dig into my chest, piercing my armor deep enough to draw blood. Due to the proximity of the wolf, I was unable to get a full swing upon it with the axe, but instead shoved the blade into the great maw to prevent the saber teeth from sinking into my skull. The thing reared back reflexively, as I must have initiated a choking sensation with the axe blade. This was the opening I'd been waiting for.

I pulled the axe back and to the right before striking. With all my might, I used my forearm and wrist to swing the axe up from the side of the ferocious canine in a curving arc that ended with the blade dug into back of the wolf's neck, carving away the fur and flesh, exposing the monster's spine. This angered it further, spurring the beast to redouble its efforts to tear the armor from my breast. Just as I heard a ripping noise from the straps on the right side of my hauberk, I swung the axe again and again, striking the same spot and cutting into the spine. The fourth strike landed just as the beast moved in to sink its teeth into my now-exposed throat. With a final roar, the beast fell prone upon me, paralyzed from my final blow.

It was then the direness of my situation hit me full on. Here I was, pinned to the ground by the bulk of the ice wolf, completely unable to free myself. The smell of blood would certainly draw other predators, including the great white snow lions, which often stalked the wolves as prey in the winter months when the mastodons were seldom seen. Unfortunately for me, the giant snow cats were far from the most fearsome of predators to prowl the Nir Mountains.

I tried unsuccessfully to push the beast off me with direct force, but to no avail. Knowing I had to free myself as soon as possible, I wedged the head of the axe under the wolf's left front shoulder. I then braced the axe handle on the ground and with all my might, I pulled the handle in toward my body. The base of the handle slowly slid inward on the ice below, elevating the bulk of the beast just enough for me to wriggle free from beneath it.

Once I stood again, I noticed the sun had dipped fully behind the mountains to the west, meaning night was not far away. Knowing my pursuit for the day had ended, I was faced with finding a suitable shelter to protect myself from the freezing temperatures or die in the pass.

"Thankfully," I thought, "at least I have a meal suitable for eating." With a few well placed strikes, I hewed a massive rear leg off the wolf, tossed it over my shoulder and moved on in search of a cave or other cover to shelter in until dawn. With one last backward glance at the felled beast, I wondered if it was indeed the man-wolf so many hunters had spoken of around late night campfires when women and children were not about.

CHAPTER FOUR: *THE OLD MAN*

After leaving the scene of the wolf attack, I searched for a dozen minutes or more before coming upon a low hanging cave opening. The entrance was barely tall enough for me to crawl through, but once inside I was pleased to see the cave expanded to several times my height. I stepped forward until I was deep enough within to stand fully upright as the same warmth that filled the other caves helped pull the chill from my bones. Moving in far enough from the entrance to avoid the icy fingers of the winter winds, I lay the wolf leg down and cast about for a means to create fire. While I had tinder and steel, finding something that would burn was never easy in the frozen wastes.

I ventured further into the caves, looking for anything I might use, but found little in the immediate area. Going deeper still, I rounded a corner and came upon a ghastly scene. In a small alcove, barely large enough for several men to stand within, I found a pile of human remains nearly knee deep. The bones had been picked clean and from the looks of them, were more than dry enough to burn. I wondered if they but belonged to the souls who had gotten lost among the mountains and starved to death within the cave. Dismissing the question of where they came from and merely considering the find good fortune, I pulled as many of them as I could into my arms and returned to where I'd laid the wolf leg.

I soon had a fire burning and fashioned a make-shift spit with my long knife so that I might cook the wolf meat. As I waited for the meal to sear, the past hours events came to mind and I cursed myself for a fool. I should have considered that a wolf, or worse, a lion, might set upon my path. My determined focus on my goal had made me sloppy and it had nearly cost me my life. Were I to die, Lacina would have no hope of rescue, instead she would most assuredly endure the torture and depravity the Yslings mete upon their prey until her beautiful body could stand no more. The very idea of my love experiencing such hardships caused my flesh to crawl and the blood in my veins to rush through my ears.

Tomorrow, if the gods smiled upon me, I would overtake the Yslings and have my revenge. The idea of saving Lacina and avenging my clan brought a slight snarl to my lips.

As I sunk my teeth into the first bits of meat, enjoying the sustenance, a noise in front of me brought my head up and with it came the axe, at the ready. While I knew most creatures feared fire and shied away from it at all costs, the events of the last two days prevented me from letting my guard down now. To this end, I had kept the axe upon my lap while I attempted to devour my meal.

In front of me, just on the opposite side of the fire he stood. A skin wrapped skeleton of an old man, dressed in rags, his empty flesh hanging from his bones as if nothing filled the void between them. I found myself recoiling ever so slightly, completely taken off guard by the oldster. A fearsome predator bent on taking my meal and my life, I would expect out here in the wilderness. A decrepit, half-starved old man I did not.

For what seemed like a thousand years we stared at one another in utter silence. My mind, completely unable to fathom a scenario that would

THE BONES HAD BEEN PICKED CLEAN...

logically place the old man here, now, simply ran through and rejected a dozen reasons why the malnourished elder might be intruding upon my meal.

Finally, I spoke. "What do you want?" the gruffness of my voice grated through the empty cavern, invading the silence like a predator in a sheep's pen.

"M-meat…" he replied, which brought my attention to his mouth and the trickle of saliva that escaped it. Surely, he was starving and here I sat, warily guarding more food than I could possible consume at once. I eyed him up and down, and once assured he posed no threat that I could discern, I spoke.

"Sit, old man. Enjoy this sumptuous flesh and tell me how it is you came to be here."

I handed him a portion of the wolf's leg, cut from the thigh with my long knife. It was more than a meal for man of his size, yet he set upon it and finished it off ere I had a chance to cut another chunk for myself.

"M-more… please."

And with that, I cut him another slice, and another. As he devoured each morsel, I stared into his eyes, watching as the meal seemed to reinvigorate him.

"You would dine with me, yet decline to answer my curiosity?"

In response to those words, he seemed to come out of a trance and looked me square in the eye for the first time since our initial meeting. The look of ravenousness was now gone, replaced by what appeared to be the piercing gaze of great intelligence.

"Please. Please forgive me… A-and thank you for sharing this. It has been too long since I've been able to eat my fill," he began, obviously feeling satisfied with the warm meal. "My name is An'kar, and my people used to rule this land… *before*."

I gnawed away on a sizeable chunk of flesh as I considered the old man's words. In hindsight, I was once again failing to see the danger before me as I looked on to what I wanted. I'm thankful I learned my lesson in this regard, as all too often in those years, I should have given up my life for it.

"'Before?' Before what?" I muttered in between chewing and swallowing the wolf meat.

"Before the ice came. Before the great volcano beneath our feet drew silent. Before this once fertile land became a frozen waste."

"I've heard stories of the time before the ice came, but thought them merely legends…"

"Oh, no. Legends are myth, fantasy, stories told to entertain the imaginative… what I speak is truth. For centuries we lived in the mountains and valleys, taking bountiful sustenance from the land. We raised livestock, farmed a wide variety of food stuffs and engaged in wonderful pastimes of poetry, painting, sculpture and song. We lived a blessed life, that's for sure."

"You keep saying we. Surely, this time you speak of is thousands of years gone. Am I to believe that you are equally as old?"

"Sadly, yes," he replied, with a still born tear welling across the bottom of his right eyelid. "I am the last of my people. My wife and children, brothers, sisters, friends and the rest of my family are all gone now. Dust to dust as they say…" his voice trailed off wistfully as it seemed he lost himself in memories of times long past.

"How is it, then, that you are still here, still breathing and eating my food?"

"Is it true? Are you the son of the Runemaster?"

The sudden change of topic threw me for a moment as I wondered how he knew of my heritage. Then he motioned ever so slightly with his index finger to my father's axe, which was lying across my knees.

"I was, until he went to The Grand Hall of the Gods two days ago. Now *I* am the Runemaster."

"I see…" he replied coyly before continuing. "I too, am the son of a great man. My father was our people's high priest. The blessings of the gods came through him to our people. When he took over for his father before him, he was full of self-sacrificing ideals. He was driven to take our people to new heights of prosperity. For, even a seemingly perfect people can look to improve their condition, no?"

It was then I noticed a change in his visage, as if events from long ago cast an ancient shadow upon his very soul. His sunken, blue eyes sparkled with a fire I'd not seen in him to this point and his hollow cheeks seemed to flush with a newfound life.

"This unquenchable zeal was a blessing in his younger years, as he found new ways for us to prosper, new methods of living that brought greater ease and comfort to our lives. His efforts ushered us into an unparalleled golden age, unlike any we had ever seen.

"But then, the flaw of his character, of all our character, shone through. His inability to be satisfied with his blessings was what did it. I'm sure of it. In fact, I'd stake my life, such as it is, on it. Having had millennia to contemplate it, I believe it to be as undeniably factual as the rock above our head and frost beyond the caverns."

"Are you speaking of hubris?" I asked, while finishing up my meal.

"No, no, of course not," he continued. "I don't believe it was ever about any-thing as petty as ego. Or at least not self-serving ego. I think he truly believed we were owed the life of the gods. To live as they do, to never have to toil again.

"And that's when it happened... he went too far, pushed too hard, demanded too much.

"And the gods became-

"ANGRY!"

His sudden, uncharacteristic outburst tensed my muscles and I invol-untarily lifted the axe from my lap, prepared to strike him down should he make one move toward me.

"Oh dear me... sorry. Didn't mean to frighten you child."

"I am anything but a child."

"To one who has lived since before your clan was ever born, you are. But, I apologize. I certainly meant no offense. "

"None taken. Please continue."

"Yes, yes. Thank you," he apologized before moving on with his tale.

"I was just becoming a man myself when the wrath fell upon us. In one mighty breath, the Nir expelled a great blackness into the air. Rivers of molten rock poured down its sides and fires consumed all signs of veg-etation. Once the eruption was over, all that was left was the dense black cloud cover which blotted out the sun, ushering in times of intense cold. The ground hardened, the animals died and soon, *all* that we had left was each other - for better or worse.

"The sun. The life giving, glowing warm light that meant everything to us, fled from our sight. At first it was obscured by the ash plumes, then those were replaced by storm clouds and peals of deafening thunder. Within days, our idyllic world was transformed into what you see before you now. Cold, lifeless, frozen and desolate.

"My father, ever refusing to bend to the will of the gods, went to his altar once more and demanded a reckoning. He would challenge them once and for all, to seize their power for our own. In this, yes, you may think he exhibited great hubris as you suggested. But, I tell you his was a righ-teous anger; the anger of a man who refused to accept his subjugation at the hands of higher powers.

"Alas, it was over ere it even began. A small portal opened in the clouds over head, and through it descended one lone crow. The raven was a mes-senger, sent from the gods to deliver our final judgment. Our people, convicted of following my father and allowing him to anger the gods, were cast into the pit. My family shared a similar fate. Within moments, only my father and I remained.

"It was then they offered the bargain. One my father grudgingly accepted in order to spare my life."

"And, what bargain was this, old man? It surely wasn't one that bode well for you, from appearances…"

"No, it did not. But, at the time, my father believed it was his only choice. Would that he had felt otherwise…"

With that, the old man stood up and turned, as if to leave. It was then that I noticed, for a third time, my inobservance and how it placed my life in the balance. Standing before me now was no old bag of bones, but a well muscled figure imbued with a physique rivaling my own. Without even thinking, I let a curse slip through my teeth.

"By the blood…"

With that utterance, the old man spun around. Except what met my eyes was no old man. Instead, standing there was fully endowed fighting man in his prime. To make matters worse, his teeth had grown into horrid fangs, and his fingernails were now obsidian claws similar to that of the ice wolf. His nose had taken on a dog-like appearance and his ears were transforming into pointed flaps of skin that aimed directly upward. It seems the tales of a wolf man who stalked the lost souls in the Nir canyons were true. But, whether I believed the stories or not, I had never thought I'd face him myself.

These observations and thoughts shot through my mind in an instant, but that was all the time the creature needed to lunge at me, claws slashing and jaws slathering.

CHAPTER FIVE: *CARNIVORE*

I dove to the side, barely escaping the beast's snapping jaws and gruesome claws that tore through the air where I had just sat only a moment prior. It chased me with swiping talons, ripping emptiness just a hairs breadth from my flesh. Hoping to regain my composure and face the thing on even footing, I retreated around the fire until I was directly opposite of where I had just stood. The beast feinted to the left, then to the right, obviously afraid of the flames, but hungry for my blood. We reached a momentary stalemate which allowed me to get my wits about me.

The creature stood a full head taller than the old man it had recently been. Its chest was hairless, but a coarse, black fur had overtaken its arms, legs and shoulders. I barely noted what looked to be a tail hanging between its legs, swishing back and forth like that of a dog on the hunt. The eyes had changed to a blood red and blazed with a piercing ferocity I don't think I'd ever witnessed before.

I reached up to draw a weapon and grasped nothing but empty air. Then my eyes fell upon my next mistake: my father's axe lay on the ground behind the snarling thing's form. Without wasting an instant, I drew my long knife and set my jaw. The wolf-man, realizing I was faster than it first anticipated, examined me with eyes that burned with a feral ferocity tempered with intelligence. That the creature was somehow still hungry I had no doubt, and that it meant to make me its next meal was equally apparent.

We circled the fire, each trying to find an opening in the other's defense. I waved the long knife back and forth until I was able to come to a halt above my father's axe. Contemplation of retrieving it was soon discarded as I realized the beast would close the distance between us before I could lift the weapon from the cavern floor. With it in my hand, I could strike the wolf-man from a distance without allowing it into my guard. But with the long knife, I was sure to open myself to the creature's teeth and claws.

The beast-man howled with an intensity that would curdle the blood of weaker men. The sound brought a memory of the pile of bones I'd found earlier and I wondered how many souls had suffered that sound as the last they ever heard. Not being one to let anything intimidate me, I replied in kind with a Kirwall war cry that caught the beast by surprise, as noted by its flaring nostrils and dilating eyes. The beast's head drew back and tilted to the left slightly, as if it were rethinking its initial judgment of my ability to challenge it. While I had given the beast pause, I knew the longer this dragged on, the greater the chance the thing would dine on my flesh before the morning sun rose.

Thinking quickly, I kicked out at the fire, scooping a flaming bone from the blaze and sending it straight at the beast's face. As the monster swatted the bone aside in an explosion of sparks and embers, I reached down and wrapped my fingers around the familiar haft. Before I could stand back up, the monster lunged across the fire at me. I had only enough time to swing the axe upward, aiming for the gullet. The blade bit deep into the belly of the beast, but its impetus carried it full upon me and we tumbled over backward, into the darkness…

+++

My shoulder hit the rock floor first, and pain shot through my frame, like a shattered window. As if he could sense my injury, the monster pressed his assault as we continued rolling backward and downward. I was previously unaware of the hole that we'd fallen into, but judging from the amount of times we rolled and bounced, I assumed it to be at least three times deeper than I was tall. As we tumbled, the beast's claws ripped across my exposed flesh more than once. We landed on the floor of the hole and once the blinding white flash from the impact left my vision, I realized we were encapsulated in total darkness. The landing separated us from one another, but by how far I was unable to ascertain. Once the ringing in my ears faded, I listened intently for any sound the beast might make.

What seemed like an eternity passed before the faintest sound of breathing caught my ear. I guessed the beast to be off to my left and far from reach. The sound of a swiping paw went past from right to left as the monster swung wildly, hoping to catch me unawares. I moved backward slowly, listening to its exertions as it sought to systematically sweep the pit with ferocious, mighty swings that would surely knock me from my feet were one to connect. The thing finally managed to back me into a corner, where I rubbed my left arm against the wall while trying to retreat further, hoping for some of the light above to shine down into this stygian pit.

I was cornered! The slathering jaws of the monster smacked together involuntarily, as the gnashing of his teeth and violent hyper-ventilating drew closer and closer. While I didn't want to swing wildly and waste what little energy I had left, my instincts screamed at me to fight back. But how was I to do that when I had no way of seeing my target? One misplaced swing would open me up to a deathblow and then all would be lost.

It was at that moment I became aware of a wound on my left bicep, where I had impacted the rock on my way down. A slight smile played across my lips as I remembered the effects my father's axe had when a healing spell was cast. Quickly, I lifted the axe head to the wound. I whispered the Old Runish incantation under my breath and pulled the blade away quickly. The runes on the blade glowed briefly, bathing the wolf man in a pale blue glimmer. He turned toward the sudden explosion of light with a snarl and then the light faded away.

Gauging the creature's distance and speed, I swung the axe with all my might. I was rewarded with the feel of the impact and muted yelp from the beast as warm fluid splattered across my face and arms. Rapidly muttering the incantation once more, the glow from the runes returned briefly, allowing me to locate the wolf-man and swing upon him once more. The second blow was enough to silence the seemingly immortal creature once and for all.

It took several more incantations to find a way back up and out of the hole – and might take even more to heal all my newfound cuts and bruises, but I soon stood next to the fire. My flesh and bones ached from the battle, but it was not enough to keep my mind from returning to my quest. While I knew I could not brave the night outside the cave, the idea of restful sleep was nothing more than a memory after the encounter with the man-wolf. Looking about, I found a nook I could rest within and easily see anything that might come upon me. Settling into the alcove, I laid the axe across my chest and was soon overcome with sleep.

CHAPTER SIX: *FEVER DREAMS*

She was there. Just beyond my outstretched hand. Yet try as I might, I could not reach her. She seemed troubled, distressed by the unknown. This stirred something within me, something disturbing and anxious. A need to comfort her, to protect her, to hold her warm, tender flesh in mine arms once more. A yearning for us to be one.

A stillborn cry died on my lips, "Lacina."

I strained forward until it seemed as if my very soul would tear loose from my body or whatever it was that anchored me to the cold, hard ground, yet despite fighting with every ounce of my essence, I could not move.

A swirling darkness enveloped her, clouding my vision and obscuring her sultry form until all that I could see was the agonized expression in her eyes as her lips pursed together to form a scream that carried my name.

Redoubling my effort to get to her only seemed to make matters worse, as she slid further away, deeper into the dark mists. For what seemed like an eternity, she slipped deeper and deeper into the stygian vapors until, with one final scream, she disappeared altogether.

My soul writhed in agony for what felt like eternity until her image was replaced with another. That of Tristan Angivar.

My fingers reached outward, as my hand trembled from an insatiable desire. Every muscle in my body tensed nearly to the point of breaking my own bones as I was overcome by a soul-grinding need to crush the life from his foul heart.

+++

A sudden gasp ripped through my lungs as I bolted upright from against the rock wall where I'd lain for the past while. My unfamiliar surroundings and tattered memories of the fever dream left my nostrils flared, eyes dilated and muscles aching as the icy sweat dripped from my frame. I was overcome with a desire to flee the cave immediately and continue my pursuit of Tristan and the Yslings. However, common sense prevailed once I spied the darkness outside the cavern and felt a brief icy wind blow through the cave mouth. No, rushing headlong into the frozen darkness would do my beloved Lacina no good at all. I turned to the still crackling fire and extended my cold hands towards it. Steam rose from my frame as the sweat evaporated in the warmth of the burning bones. As I struggled to cast the last of the dream visions from the forefront of my mind, my eyes fell upon the remains of the wolf leg. Wasting no time, I devoured my share of the meat and felt the animal's strength flow into me. After I'd had my fill, I turned and looked at the cave entrance once more. The faint glow of the rising sun was just beginning to invade the domain of darkness outside. Without a second though, I gathered my weapons and left the cave, once again on the trail of those who had slain my clan.

CHAPTER SEVEN: *COLD PURSUIT*

By mid-morning, my jogging pace had allowed me to gain significant ground on the Yslings. As I carefully peered over the top of a rise in the trail, I spotted their rear guard not more than a half hour walk in front of me. There appeared to be six of the stout warriors, moving along at a normal marching pace. Father had taught me the Yslings always had a rear guard, a group of six to ten warriors who trailed behind the main group, so as to fend off any threats that might seek to assault the war party from behind. That this was one such example of their rear guard, I had no doubt.

Every few moments, the warrior in the very rear would turn around and scan the path behind them, while the flankers peered up at the valley walls. Try as I might, I could spot no place to hide from their prying eyes if I were to abandon my vantage point. Should I try and close the gap at a dead sprint, they would surely see me with plenty of time to alert the main group. Brash as I was, even I knew better than to wade into a pack of Ysling warriors who vastly outnumbered me single-handedly. The six I could see now I felt I could defeat, the scores of others ahead of them would spell my doom, however, if I allowed even one member of the rear guard to warn them.

While mourning our dead was never the way of Clan Kirwall, as we celebrated their entry into The Grand Hall of the Gods, it was at that moment that I felt an acute stab of soulful pain at the loss of my friend Runolf. Were he still by my side, I would not hesitate in attacking the Yslings head on. And, he would gain some sense of revenge in taking as many of them to the grave as the gods would allow. Alas, it was not to be so. No, I needed a better strategy for there would be no one left to save Lacina should I fall beneath an Ysling sword. While she was a shield-maiden, and one of the most feared in all the land, neither of us held much hope in overcoming the small Ysling army apart from one another.

As I scanned the valley for any signs of a way to ambush the rear guard, my eyes fell upon what appeared to be a nest of sorts, high up the eastern wall. At that very moment, the Ysling flanker spotted it as well. He gesticulated toward the nest and after a moment's deliberation; the group took off ahead at a brisk jog. Whatever they saw, gave them reason to accelerate their pace, which meant I would need to do the same lest I fall further behind.

However, before taking off after my quarry, it seemed only prudent to discover what had spooked them. Placing my hands above my eyes to shield them from the dazzling light that reflected off of everything around, I strained to peer through the Nir mists. In the nest, I spotted two cubs playfully pouncing upon one another in mock battle. While the offspring were hardly anything to fear, the absence of their parents brought forth uneasiness in me that I once again might be skirting the line between predator and prey. If the mother was about, she was hunting for food so that her litter would grow strong enough to fend for themselves. If the father was still part of the den, he was protecting his territory. And, whether her or him I was either food or threat to one of the full-grown beasts.

The idea of a snow lion, male or female, hunting me through this frozen valley brought forth an instinct of uneasiness from the core of my soul, placed there when the world was young and my clan un-thought of. Perhaps I was better off taking my chances back within the caverns?

Casting about, I quickly realized the caves were not an option as I could spy no entrance anywhere near me. After a few moments' contemplation, it was clear there was no other choice but to stick close to the west wall and hope to move past without alerting the snow lions to my presence. Moving as rapidly as I could without drawing undue attention my way, my path veered off to the west wall. Keeping my back to it, whilst focusing alternately between the way the Yslings had gone and the snow lion nest, I moved quickly, as if death itself were stalking me – which it may very well have been.

Ere long I'd exited the narrow pass and could see the rear guard once again. Thankfully, it seemed they hadn't gained as much ground on me as I'd feared. Up ahead of them by an hour or so march, was the final pass before they descended into the valley that bordered the Bay of Abiathar. Named after an ancient priest, the bay was the only logical point of entrance to mainland for the Yslings. It was but a week's sail due west from the Bay to Osherah, their ancestral home.

If I could catch the rear guard unawares before they descended into the valley, they would have no way of alerting the main group before I dispatched them all. While I was well aware the odds were greatly against me, the idea of spilling Ysling blood brought a smile to my face and renewed my energy. Grabbing a handful of snow to slake my thirst, I re-doubled my efforts to catch the rear guard just as the main group began their descent.

The next few hours remained somewhat uneventful. I was clearly gaining ground on them, even with the occasional need to drop to one knee so the warrior who brought up the rear would not spot me on his periodic scans. I took pride in the idea that their very reason for existence was to stop an enemy from approaching unawares from behind, yet here I was closing the gap at a rapid pace.

Before long, I could see the main force of Yslings off in the distance, out ahead of the rear guard. They appeared to be as far ahead of the guard as I was to the rear. It wouldn't be long before my time to strike was at hand. Trying to navigate time by the beating of my heart, I'd counted to nearly a thousand when the main group began their descent to the Bay of Abiathar. Only a few moments longer and my blade would once again taste Ysling flesh.

Within a hundred or so beats of my pounding heart, the last of the main force crested the hilltop and descended from view. I'd timed my approach almost perfectly and was now within a few staff lengths of the warrior tasked with guarding their rear; he turned and saw me approaching. Knowing it was now or never, I quickly whispered the berserker spell and then hurled my Father's axe with all my might. The hefty steel head sunk completely through the Ysling's skull, splitting it in twain before the handle caught up and collided with his breast plate.

The kill was almost silent and would have been had the haft of mine weapon not struck his armor. However, before the five in front could react, I was among them like a wild dog let loose in a pack of house cats. Grabbing

the axe from the dead warrior's body, I swung with a ferocity born of growing anger that welled within me the longer my pursuit continued.

The second Ysling's body dropped to his right as his head flew to the left,
and third fared no better as I spun around bringing my axe into his neck
with both hands, severing his skull and sailing it into the fifth warrior. The
fourth, trying to slip behind me, struck a glancing blow that slid off my
shoulder plate and logged for the briefest of instants in the gap between
my forearm plate and my chain mail. The momentum of his swing pulled
me off-balance just enough to spare the life of the sixth Ysling, as my axe
cleaved the air inches from his face in a mighty arc that should have parted
the top of his head from the bottom.

In the same instant, the fifth warrior regained his composure and
jumped at me, driving downward with his sword in a stroke meant to end
my life. Unfortunately for him, he struck empty air as the sword of his
compatriot kept me from entering the space where he'd aimed his sword,
call it luck, or call it divine intervention, but it was all I needed to complete my task.

Kicking outward with my right leg, I slammed my foot into the fifth
Ysling's gut, which sent him crashing backward into the sixth. Reversing
my momentum, I brought the axe upward from near my feet and caught
the fourth assailant in the chin, shattering it in a splash of teeth, blood and
bone as the axe continued its upward trajectory and sliced his face in half.

Spinning once more, I leapt upon the fifth and sixth, who were trying
to regain their feet after I'd knocked them down a heartbeat earlier. Two
quick, decisive blows put an end to their opposition. I spun around yet
again, looking for another Ysling warrior, turning from side to side several times before realizing all six were dead, their lifeblood staining the
ivory snow.

It took several deep breaths to allow the rushing in my ears to subside
as the effects of the battle lust ran their course. Using control techniques
taught me by my Father, I slowed my heartbeat, mastered my breathing and
kneeled to thank the gods for handing me victory.

I was one step closer to rescuing Lacina and six more dead Yslings
closer to avenging my Father and our clan. Taking one final deep breath, I
cleaned the head of my Father's axe, *my axe*, in the snow and prepared to
continue pursuing the main Ysling force.

Just as I began to renew my pursuit, the sound I'd dreaded for the last
few hours struck my ears.

RRROOOOOOOAAAAAAARRRRRRRRRRR!!!!

CHAPTER EIGHT: *THE WHITE DEATH*

It was my eighth spring, Runolf and I, having completed our learning and chores for the day, which included helping plant the fall harvest, engaged in a game Kirwall boys had played for centuries. Closing my eyes, I counted twenty heartbeats silently, then opening them, I would play the role of the White Death and stalk Runolf, until I was able to pounce upon him, "devouring" him and thus ending the round.

We had played this game so many times, Runolf's hiding places had become routine. Behind the wheat stalls, ducked alongside the horse troughs or lying prone under one of the Long Houses. These were the places I would find Runolf, pounce upon him, pretend to devour him the way we imagined the White Death would, and then we'd laugh and start all over, with Runolf playing the role of hunter while I hid from the deadly fate.

With the horse troughs standing between our starting point and the Long Houses, I presumed to check there first. Sneaking up until I was able to jump around the corner, hoping to catch Runolf by surprise. I leapt into view, or at least where I expected he would be, but to my surprise, no one was hiding there.

Then I moved from Long House to Long House, checking under the one his family called home, then Lacina's, the Great House where my family lived and all the rest. From house to house I moved, each time jumping into view expecting to startle Runolf prior to pouncing upon him. And, from house to house I moved without seeing him.

At long last, there remained just one place left, the wheat stalls on the other side of the village from whence we started.

Tiring of the game by this point, I gave up any pretense of stealth and ran to the wheat stalls, preparing to jump upon Runolf and devour him once and for all.

Just as I was about to round the corner, I heard the loudest, most terrifying noise that had ever struck mine ears. While fear was not an emotion myself, or any other Kirwall clansman for that matter, was familiar with, the sound elicited a feeling of great unease within me. It was at that moment that I truly understood that our world, Njordica, was home to things far more powerful than the men and women of our village.

As I came into view of the nightmare, I noted Runolf was between it and I, on his bottom, trying desperately to back-pedal away from the thing's slathering jaws. The look of hunger in its eyes seemed akin to insanity as it began rearing backward to jump upon poor Runolf and end him. The beast's white

...*REALIZING ALL SIX WERE DEAD.*

fur allowed the thing to blend into the snow during the winter, but with so much green about the village after the last thaw, it stood out as something greatly out of place. The lush white mane encircled its horrible face, lips snarled backward revealing several rows of dagger-like teeth. Its body rippled with muscles that were clearly possessed of strength far greater than any man.

Sounding another violent, bone-shaking cry, the thing leapt toward Runolf, massive claws extended from each front paw, as it meant to kill him before taking me next.

Time seemed to slow in that instant, as many dying folk tell of experiencing in the moments before death. I clearly recall the creature leaving the ground, achieving the pinnacle of its mighty arc then descending toward Runolf to snuff out his life once and for all.

Then, just as the monster moved past the peak of its leap, the blur struck it in the side of its mighty head, turning the face off to my right as the thing fell to the ground next to Runolf's prone form.

As time regained normal speed, my Father appeared, followed by Runolf's father and several other warriors. Bending low, Father grabbed the haft of his axe and with a mighty tug, pulled the blade free of the creature's head.

"The White Death..." Runolf's father whispered.

"This one is sickly," my Father interjected. "Notice how much smaller it is than the ones we see in the Nir Valley."

Gazing upon it with a mind no longer reeling from the nightmare, it was easy to see what Father mentioned. This snow lion was on the edge of starvation. Ribs protruded from its flanks, dead skin crusted over its lips and nostrils. This beast had clearly not eaten in quite some time. But why would it come here? So far away from the mountains and valleys they were known to hunt in?

As if reading my thoughts, Father turned to me and said "The fertile autumn followed by the harsh winter must have left too little food for the male snow lions. This fellow, I imagine, was the odd one out," he explained. "I would wager he heard the horses and came looking for an easy meal."

"But, all he found was my blade!" Runolf, now standing and appearing none the worse for wear, pretended to stab the great beast with his imaginary sword. "Die vile beast!"

A rich belly laugh sounded as Runolf's father chuckled at his son's sudden bravery. "If it were only that easy to kill the White Death, young Runolf. Half-starved they might be easy prey, but a snow lion with all of its strength is more than the equal of any two warriors of our clan, or any other for that matter."

"Were it an alpha male in his prime gone rogue," Father added. "I'm afraid even my axe blow would not have slowed the beast. Count yourself blessed by the gods, Runolf, they have seen fit to allow you to live another day."

+++

The sound ripped me from the present moment back to that day long ago, when the White Death nearly descended on Runolf. My blood ran cold as the words of Runolf's father rose from memory to haunt the present moment.

"...a snow lion with all of its strength is more than the equal of any two warriors of our clan..."

Judging from the volume of the beast's roar, it was not upon me just yet. Spinning and dropping to one knee, I held my axe before me as if its extended blade could shield me from the leap of one thousand pounds of muscle, fang and claw.

In the briefest of thoughts, I felt relieved as the creature was several body lengths away, turned slightly sideways, nostrils flared as it took in the scene of the carnage I'd wrought on the Ysling rear guard. It seemed at that moment, we shared some sort of instinctive, supernatural connection – not as predator and prey, but hunter to hunter. Tilting its head to the right, the beast let out a lesser growl, as if to test me. Without thinking, I replied with a battle cry of mine own.

YEEEAAAAAAAAAAAAAAAAAAAAA!!!

At the onset of my voice, the beast flinched ever so slightly. Clearly, it had never been challenged before by anything so much smaller than itself. The monster slowly paced back and forth, unsure of exactly what to do with me.

While all this happened in matter of seconds, for me it felt like an eternity – one in which the main Ysling force drew further and further away from me, taking my beloved Lacina with them.

Once more my mind retreated to that fateful day when the dying snow lion almost devoured Runolf.

Looking past the laughing form of my friend as he continued to parry and slash at the snow lion's corpse, I saw her. Even at that age, the very sight of her took my breath away. While I wasn't old enough to truly comprehend what it meant to be a husband, I knew I wanted her as my wife. Knew it as truly as I knew the sun rose and fell.

In hindsight, I'm sure my Father saw the look we shared, Lacina and I, for he paused a moment ere he grabbed me by the arm and sent me back to our Great House, where mother was calling us to sup.

The passion that fueled my love of Lacina welled up within me at the remembrance of that moment. And, without hesitation, I threw myself over the dead bodies, Axe held high, battle cry ripping out from deep within my lungs. I would slay this beast now, here, and resume my quest to regain Lacina's freedom or die this very day at the claws of the White Death.

The ferocity of my movement startled the snow lion once more and it reeled backward, narrowly escaping the first swipe of my axe. I found myself screaming the spell of the berserker once more, although deep down I knew it was to no avail – the spell simply would not work so soon after casting it to vanquish the Yslings.

However, something about reciting those words seemed to give me bravery, renewed strength and a will to destroy my opponent at any cost.

Realizing I was suddenly more threat than it had faced ere now, the snow lion reared up on its hind legs and swiped at me with its right foreleg. Its paw was the size of a dinner plate, with five claws, each nearly the length of my whole hand slashing through the air. In retrospect, I know not how I survived that first attack, but somehow the beast missed me altogether.

At once I ducked down and spun about, twirling my axe from on high, around in a mighty circle and back into the path of the monster. The swing was halted suddenly as it dug deep into the snow lion's left foreleg. A cry the likes of which I'd never heard before, and never again, escaped the monster's jaws and it swatted at me again with a speed that left no room for my reflexes to escape.

The next instant was a jumbled blur of motion, pain and cold before everything went black…

+++

The icy mists slipped and slid before my eyes, seeking to hide her from me. Just beyond my reach she was there, my goddess in human form, Lacina. The outsides of her lips curled upward ever so slighting in an inviting smile as she beckoned me to her with an outstretched hand. The silk, sapphire dress pulled taught across her form as the wind, crossing left to right over her body, sought to pull it from her. As her golden locks waved in the same manner as her dress, the mists swirled and eddied between us as if taunting me with what seemed just beyond my reach.

Try as I might, I could not advance towards her. With every ounce of might within me, I willed my body to draw closer to my love, but it was all for naught. Once the realization of my apparent paralysis struck me, Lacina's form began retreating into the distance, but oddly, not of her own power. In the last moment before the swirling winds obscured her from my sight, I watched as her gorgeous face was suddenly twisted from mesmerizing smile to an expression of abject terror.

+++

Awakening suddenly, I lifted my prone form from the snow, unsure of whether I yet lived or I lay in some icy antechamber awaiting admittance to The Grand Hall of the Gods. Then the pain took over, racking my head and face as it sought to relive the last moments of consciousness ere the White Death laid me low.

Of the fact the creature had indeed landed a death blow upon me I was quite certain. Why I remained alive was a mystery. As I strove to regain my feet, I looked around, noting my surroundings. All about were the bodies of the Ysling rear guard, just as the fatal wounds I'd inflicted on them had left them; their blood covered the snow, contrasting crimson against pure white.

But, there was something else…

At first, I couldn't make out what it was, until my memories returned fully. It would seem my blow into the snow lion's left foreleg dug deeper than I'd thought, severing the limb from the beast. The detached leg lay near the edge of the battle site, with the rear of the creature just beyond. Standing to my full height I could see the beast must have turned to seek refuge after it felled me, but the loss of blood from the severed limb was too much for it to overcome. The creature bled out mere feet from where it knocked me unconscious, thankfully.

It was then that my mind re-focused on the task at hand: rescuing my beloved Lacina. The thought of my fever dream sent my heart racing and the surge of energy brought with it cleared the haze from my thoughts. How long had I been down, I wondered? Based on steam still rising from the snow lion's blood, I surmised it had been mere moments. Quickly, I looked through the Ysling's packs to seek any sustenance they might have and secured it in Runolf's pack, still slung over my shoulders. In a moment of inspiration, I grabbed one of their shields from the snow and slung it on my back.

Wasting no time, I raced to the top of the hill, hoping to spy the main Ysling force down below as they descended to the Bay of Abiathar.

While hope burned in my heart, what my eyes told me once I was able to see the path below dashed it against the rocks once more.

CHAPTER NINE: *ESCAPE!*

The path from the top of the rise I stood upon, down to the water's edge was easily an hour's march. A fit, well-rested man might make it in thirty minutes. In my current condition, my mind believed I could do the latter, but the exhaustion that was setting in on my physical self embraced the former.

As my eyes swept downward to the water's edge, I could see the small fleet of long boats the Yslings had used to travel to the Nir mainland from their frozen hell of a home, Osherah. Father had once told me it was an effect of the currents, both water and air, that pulled frigid temperatures from the farthest northern regions down across Osherah; the island had no other season than winter due to strange phenomenon. Once the wind and tidal streams met the Sea of Ashgul that separated Osherah and Nir, the warm waters from the south removed some of the bitter cold before the currents moved along the continental coast and the winds blew inward. The Sea of Ashgul was known as some of the most violent waters in all of Njordica, with incessant storms. Few aside from the Yslings could easily navigate these waters without great loss of life.

With all that in mind, I had driven myself tirelessly to catch Lacina's captors and free her before they could return to the turbulent waters and make good their escape back to accursed Osherah. But, the sight before me eradicated that hope.

Down below, I spied the remaining Ysling force, my first real view of them in their entirety since this all began a few days ago. From what I could tell, there appeared to be only about fifty of the hellspawn still alive. It gave me the briefest of smiles as I realized my kinsman and I had taken down roughly three-quarters of their invasion force, despite their duplicity and the element of surprise they had upon us.

All but a handful were already aboard their long boats, preparing to put out to sea. The final batch was seeming to have some sort of commotion preventing them from boarding. Knowing I needed a closer look, I broke into a full sprint, then leaped outward and landed in the snow atop the

Ysling shield I'd stolen from the downed rear guard. I was able to slide quite a distance on it before coming to a halt. As I drew closer to the Yslings, I was able to make out the source of the commotion on the beach. It seemed my dear Lacina had managed to separate an Ysling from their sword and was determined to make a stand. Employing the sword skills taught to her by our parents, the shield maiden wove a web of death about her, parting the first Ysling nearest her from his head, then leaping and twirling into a group of three more, where she cut limb from torso, legs from hips and jaw from skull before the rest could even react.

In what seemed like the blink of an eye, she had already downed several of the Yslings as the rest had backed her against a rocky outcropping. Like a pack of jackals seeking to take down a wounded tigress, they feinted at her from side to side and about the front, seeking a hole in her guard that they simply couldn't find.

It was then my eyes fell upon another figure, who had returned to the beach from one of the long boats. He slunk around behind Lacina as I was helpless to do anything other than continue sliding down the hillside on the stolen shield. Once behind her, he mounted the outcropping and reached down and grabbed her bodily from behind.

I let out a cry to alert her, but the sea winds shoved my voice back at me in an unrelenting manner. I was helpless to do anything other than watch it all unfold. My Lacina had taken an accounting for her life and hopefully, they still saw enough value to not end her this very moment.

Pinning her arms to her side, the assailant managed to surprise Lacina and disarm her. Prepared for his actions, several of the Ysling warriors jumped on my love and bound her hands and feet. As they lifted her above their heads and proceeded to carry her to the boat, I finally got a clear enough view of the man who had subdued her. Of course, it was him, that vile cur of a traitor, Tristan. But now, he no longer wore the crest of Kirwall and our clan armor, which explained why I'd not recognized him immediately. Instead he was adorned in the warriors' garb of the Yslings. It would seem his betrayal of our clan was now complete.

As I continued my rapid descent, stopping only long enough to dislodge the shield when it caught into a particular patch of ice or protruding rock, before leaping forward once more, I watched helplessly as the Yslings boarded their long boats and set out into the violent, white-capped waters. Any hope I had of keeping them from taking my beautiful Lacina from our homeland was now gone. One by one the remaining members of the Ysling force set out to sea. It was then that I thanked the gods so many of the enemy warriors now lay dead upon our shores. For they'd had to leave behind enough long boats to ferry well over a hundred back across the frozen sea. This meant a way for me to pursue them, even if I must travel to the ends of the world and back again.

They were closing on the horizon when my descent ended on the beach. The massive waves of the Bay of Abiathar obscuring most of their fleet from my view. Grabbing supplies from several of the long boats, I loaded up one which seemed to be the stoutest of the remaining ships, yet easiest for one man to maneuver. While intended to have a crew of dozens of oarsmen and one helmsman, the long boats of nearly every northern tribe were also designed to allow only one person to sail them, in case only one man remained from a raiding party.

It took all my remaining strength to dislodge the slender vessel from the beach and get it back into the surf. Thankfully the swirling winds had changed direction and now poured down the hill from whence I came, pushing the air, and my sail, out to seas. This, I took, to be a blessing of the gods. Before long I was beyond the surf and out into the water, leaving behind everything I'd ever known in pursuit of everything I yearned for.

All northerners were well adapted to the sea. By the time I was eight winters old Father had taken me out into Kirwall Loch more times than I could recall. He taught me to control a ship on my own, and command a ship crewed with mighty oarsmen. How to navigate by stars, read the tides and follow the schools of fish that migrated below the surface.

Most importantly, he taught me to beware the monsters below that preyed on those fish – and anything else that was unlucky enough to venture into their hunting waters.

By now, the sun was fading behind the Nir Mountains at my back. While I was only catching brief glimpses of the rearmost ships in the Ysling fleet at this juncture, thankfulness once again washed over me. If the Nir Mountains weren't blocking the sun's rays from shining out from horizon to horizon, my lone long boat would stand out, silhouetted in the distance for the entire Ysling fleet to spy. As it were, the angle of the suns waning light would create a myriad of illusions and reflections on the surging waves all around me, hiding my pursuit from the prying eyes of my enemies.

If the gods were with me, (and why wouldn't they be? Clan betrayal was one of the worst sins imaginable), my maiden voyage across the Sea of Ashgul would take no more than a week. Now it was time to plan my strategy. If I was able to close on the fleet just enough, I could overtake them before they were able to make it inland to their clan lands. If not, well, I wasn't opposed to dispatching the entire accursed clan to their afterlife, or more preferably, Hel.

After traveling a great distance into the night, my exhaustion set in. Lashing the tiller to stay the course with a series of ropes, then wrapping another rope around my torso and tying it off on one of the oarsman benches lest I get tossed overboard in an instant by the rough seas, I allowed the rolling waves to lull me to sleep.

CHAPTER TEN: *LEVIATHAN!*

Through the roiling fog she beckoned me. Straining to move towards her captivating form, I felt as if I were walking in chest deep snows. Every inch forward required soul-draining effort worsened by the sight my eyes beheld: try as I might, my beautiful Lacina grew further and further from me. I looked on, helplessly as she seemed to walk out upon icy, still waters. Puzzled, my mind sought to unwrap the riddle of just what was happening. She beckoned me closer yet retreated further from my reach. With every ounce of strength left in me I reached for her, and then, Lacina began to sink beneath the water's surface and my heart sank with her. I strained forward with everything in me until a mighty impact seemed to shake the entire world around me. And, in an instant, she was gone into the depths…

+++

Bolting upright from my sleep, I gathered my wits about me, somewhat confused by my surroundings. It had been many winters since I'd slept overnight on a long boat and the reality of the rolling seas were unexpected in my first waking moments. However, within seconds the events of the past few weeks came rushing back. The violent jerk that woke me from my dreams – was that merely something concocted by my imagination or-

THUNK!

That thought died before I could complete it. The entire long boat seemed to jostle upward a few fingers from the impact. Assuming I was striking some rocky formation, or particularly nasty piece of flotsam, I looked over the side to see if I could ascertain the source of the impact. While the sun had yet to rise, the moon's waning light cast broken rays from between the clouds overhead, making it hard to see much below the surface of the turbulent waters.

THUNK!

By now, I was fairly certain the boat wasn't striking anything, rather something was striking it! The Sea of Ashgul was home to a seemingly unending array of legendary creatures. From the dragon sharks who could devour an entire man in one bite with their thousand toothed maws, to the hydroctopai, a creature with eight heads – each possessing eight fang-filled mouths, and eight claw laden tentacles longer than any three men were tall. These horrific creatures, according to legend, could drag a long boat into the depths all by themselves, and to make it worse, they swam in predatory schools with up to a dozen full grown monstrosities attacking entire fleets at once.

THUNK!

My imagination ran wild due to my inability to spy whatever horror was seeking to upend the long boat. But, my will asserted itself and started seeking a way to overcome this new threat. It was then I determined the pattern of the creature's attacks: when the ship was upon the crest or rising and falling on the swells of the mighty waves, it seemed to be out of reach of the thing which attacked from the depths. It was only when my craft descended into the valleys between waves that the horror from below would seek to end my journey.

This thought galvanized my actions, and wasting no time, I unlashed the tiller and changed course to ride upon the crest of a great wave coming up from behind. At first, I was unsure just how long I could keep the long boat on the wave, before either slipping behind it and into the monster's reach or rolling off the front, which would certainly capsize the craft. However, after what felt like an eternity, I realized the assault had abated and my new course brought with it a modicum of respite.

But a moment was all I'd gained. As they're prone to do, the great wave overtook another, smaller wave, nigh splitting the larger one in half. It was then I found myself descending into another valley between crests.

Tink-tack-tck-bak

This new series of sounds was nothing like the prior assault on the hull. Casting my vision over the side again, I saw what appeared to be pieces of another long boat cast about in the waves.

Th-thud-ud

And three bodies!

This new assault on the hull wasn't from splintered pieces of the long boat however, these were water-logged corpses of Ysling warriors! The monster below had managed to fell at least one of the ships I pursued! My heart began to race as I feared my lovely Lacina had joined them and my dream had been prophetic!

The further I cast my gaze, the larger the debris field appeared to be. Thankfully, the majority of it was concentrated in an area not much larger than a long house. This told me two things: the monster had only managed to destroy one of the Yslings' craft and the assault hadn't happened much before I sailed into it's path. The tides and winds would certainly scatter the wreckage across miles of open water given time, but for now, it was still contained in a small area.

Catching glimpses between surges of wind and wave I spied a dozen Ysling bodies in total. Knowing their long boats were designed to carry exactly twelve warriors gave me a sense of peace: my Lacina was not on this ill-fated ship, but another that had hopefully escaped the wrath of this monster of the sea.

THUNK!

What a fool I was! In my desire to discern Lacina's fate, I'd allowed the long boat to linger in the watery valley, and the path of the beast below. And, this time, it would seem I'd pay for my tactical indiscretion. The noise brought with it a sharper, secondary sound, the kind that accompanies cracking wood. Looking to the hull, I saw the damage; the creature had managed to sever the joint between the center line and the first starboard plank. With nothing to employ as a patch for the leaking wound in the ship's centerline, I knew immediately the fate of my craft was to be the same as the one I'd just passed.

Grabbing some unused rope from the deck box, I forced it into the widening crack as a means of temporarily slowing the incoming water. Knowing this was a short-lived fix at best, I prepared myself for the inevitable battle to come. But, I was a Runemaster, not a fish. My battle skills worked best on dry ground or standing atop the deck of a ship. I'd never once fought below the waves and for a moment doubted my effectiveness in that arena.

Determined to fight the monster on my terms, I turned the tiller to port in an effort to keep the boat in the valley. Looking over the side, I was finally blessed with the right angle of moonlight and waves to see what was rising up to meet me from the depths.

The horrors of the man-eating dragon shark and ship wrecking hydroctopai would have been a welcome sight compared to what my gaze fell upon.

This was neither an eating machine or school of territorial squid, oh that it were!

The bulk fast approaching me was more than twice the size of my long boat – thank the gods it had somehow been unable to capsize the vessel so far! As my eyes fell full upon it, I recognized the massive predator from tales Father had told me the very first time I'd spent a night upon the waters of Kirwall Bay. It was outlined in a shimmering blue luminescence that had led many sailors to call the thing a sea ghost.

+++

The stars glittered overhead as I absent-mindedly identified the constellations every young man must learn by my age. Seven winters I'd been upon this world, seven winters closer to manhood. Yet, I was still just a boy. Resting my head in a coil of ropes used to lash off the long boat when at dock, the silent whisper of wind was just enough to slide a slight chill across us as we slowly drifted along the dark waters.

"It is good to always have your bearings, knowing your place among the stars, my son," Father began in his deep, steely voice. "But a warrior must also remain ever-aware of what lies below."

"'Below?'" my confusion came in a reactive response I blurted without thought.

"Yes, Skarl, below."

"What do you mean, Father?"

"Before the world was old, Tridon the Brave, oldest son of the all-god, king of the seas, through his own folly as a young man, unleashed monsters unlike anything that roamed the lands," Father explained. "These foul beasts, their bulk too large to allow for quick movement on the plains or through the mountains, slithered and slipped into the waters that cover Njordica, claiming the depths for their own.

"Since that dreadful day, mighty beasts that inspire nightmares in even the stoutest of warriors, lurk below us at all times, young Skarl."

He paused for a moment, first looking up into the sky, then over the edge of the long boat and down into the deep.

"I've heard of the dragon shark," I replied, conjuring a memory of Runolf and I as one of our teachers, a shield maiden named Skadiya, taught us of how her father died from wounds incurred whilst fending off a dragon shark attack after his long boat was capsized in Kirwall Loch. A brief smile played across my lips, recalling how my best friend was so smitten with our teacher. He couldn't wait to be in her presence, dreaming that some-day she would be his wife, despite that fact she was twenty years his senior.

"Aye, the dragon shark," Father continued, pulling me back from my memories. "A monster with one purpose: to devour flesh and blood. Those horrors are just one of the many unleashed by Tridon's folly into the depths. But, there is one far more ferocious, one that even the mighty dragon sharks fear. As legends tell, the god sought to undue his mistake many years later, and with great hubris he went about creating a thing so formidable it would immediately ascend to the apex of the undersea world. Armed with thousands upon thousands of knife-like teeth, forged by Tridon's own hands to destroy the scourges of the deep, the most horrifying monster of them all, some call the sea ghost, the one truly known as *Leviathan*."

"So, I don't understand, isn't the dragon shark more powerful than all sea life, including Leviathan?"

"Oh no, young Skarl," Father shook his head. "The terror of the deep is nigh three times the size of an adult male dragon shark and would make short work of one in a direct encounter. However, the dragon shark is cunning. Normally a lone predator, it can sense blood in the water for miles and determine the origins of its prey simply from a taste of crimson stained waters. When the dragon shark is alerted to the presence of Leviathan, it summons kin to attack the great beast as one."

"Does that mean dragon sharks have clans? Like us?"

"In some ways, yes," he tried to explain. "Imagine a rogue warrior who only sought help from others when threated by a frost giant. This fighting man, knowing instinctively he could not hope to overcome the towering opponent on his own, would seek the help of a dozen or more warriors, then attack the giant as one in the hopes of swift victory."

"Then a clan of dragon sharks can kill Leviathan?"

"Perhaps…" Father's voice trailed off, leaving with it more questions than answers.

My gaze returned to the stars, but this time, as the pinpoints of light that filled the firmament above reflected in my eyes, my mind fixated on what lay below me. What horrors hide in the deep, separated from me by nothing more than a handful of hull planks? It was that night I truly learned the meaning of 'sleep with one eye open'.

+++

These recollections of youth flashed through my mind, casting a shadow of uneasiness on my very soul. It would seem this predicament was going from bad to worse. It was then a flash of inspiration struck me. If I were unable to greatly wound the mighty beast, a clan of dragon sharks might finish the job! This thought catalyzed my next actions with speed and determination.

Yanking the rope from the crack in the hull, I lifted my axe on high. My eyes went to the waters below, looking for the bluish glow from the ghost. It was but an instant before I detected it rising up to strike once again. Then timing it to coincide with the next impact, I brought my axe down into the gap with everything I had in me.

THUNK!

While the monster struck the hull once again, my axe bit into its nose with a blow that I hoped would have slain a man. The resulting spasm of pain from the thing jolted the long boat far worse than the initial impact. Lifting my axe to the sky, preparing to strike again, I noted the black ichor dripping from the blade, evidence I had struck the beast a mighty blow! Now its blood was upon the waters, a siren call for the dragon sharks, bound to be in the area already after the Ysling craft went under.

Wide-eyed and heart racing, I turned this way and that, looking for any evidence the mighty beast was returning. At the same time, I noted the next wave wall coming towards me. Wasting no time, I yanked the tiller to port, aiming the long boat upward, climbing the mountain of water as swiftly as possible, knowing this would take me out of the monsters reach for a moment or two.

Looking aftward, I watched it breach the surface where the ship had just been, getting my first sight of the gaping wound my axe had opened in its nose. The head of the beast was easily the size of the mighty double doors that once guarded the entry into our Great House. It's mouth, more than large enough to swallow me whole, dragging me to its innards where I would suffer like the legendary wizard Yonesh who was pulled from the bow of a ship by one of these horrors ages ago. As the story went, he spent several days in the belly of the beast, casting spells in an effort to escape, until the thing spat him up upon the beach, half his flesh eaten away from the digestive fluids in the creature's gullet. The very idea of finding myself inside this monster was something I chose not to indulge.

At once, as my ship was about to crest the wave, I yanked the tiller hard to port, turning back down the wave into the valley below. Based on the timing between strikes, my craft had just enough time to reach the bottom.

THUN-CRACKK!

"...DRAGON SHARKS HAVE CLANS? LIKE US?"

The monster broke the surface once again, murderous intent full upon it from the pain it endured at end of my axe. Seeking to end me once and for all, it charged the air above once more, but this time, the horror of the depths found the prow of the long boat crashing into the gaping wound in its snout.

The strangest of sounds assaulted my ears on the tail of the impact. At once I heard the now all-too-familiar sound of the beast striking my ship, married to the breaking of the bow as, driven by the rapid descent down the water wall, it drove into the monster with a force far greater than my arm could bring to bear with the axe. Before the second noise could fade, a warbling, gurgling muffled noise issued forth from the monster, one I could only assume was a scream of pain.

While my strategy certainly seemed to strike a massive blow to the beast, it also rendered my long boat nearly uncontrollable, as the planks and beams that formerly made up the prow now jutted off in unnatural directions, splintered and broken from the impact. The ship was taking on water at a far faster rate now and it wouldn't be long ere I must join the creature in the depths.

Sudden motion off the starboard side caught my attention, then more from port. Squinting to see into the dark waters, I noted the tell-tale, saw-tooth fins protruding from the depths: dragon sharks! Just how many there were I could not ascertain, as they flitted and darted below me, presumably striking the Leviathan, one by one in a coordinated attack just as Father had described during the voyage of my seventh summer.

While they seemed to have no interest in the wreckage of my long boat, the sharks continued their assault on the monster for what seemed like hours, but in recollection was probably a far shorter period of time. Knowing that to enter those water would spell certain death, and an end to my quest to free Lacina, I took the only course of action left to me. Climbing the mast until I was able to stand upon the spar that held the top of the sail aloft, I lashed myself in place, praying the gods would deliver me once more.

How long I sat upon the mast I don't recall, yet somehow, miraculously, it remained somewhat upright in the waning storm until exhaustion over-took me once more.

+++

Solid beams of light pierced the depths, separating the darkness from itself in dozens of swathes, cast down from the sky above the surface. I found myself swimming with all my might toward her, my Lacina. Her shimmering blond locks drifting about her exquisite, heart-shaped face as she reached towards me with an expression of anticipation and fear. However, the harder I tried to swim towards my love, the further from me she seemed to move. Ere long, I was unable to make out the expression on her face. Within moments, she was gone, obscured from my vision by the depths that separated us. With this, the beams of light that pierced downward from above faded away, one by one.

CHAPTER ELEVEN: *Draugr*

"Bring him aboard!" the gruff voice broke through my sleeping thoughts, waking me before my eyes opened once again. I was aware of a great light and wondered if, once fully awake, I would spy Rassful the Guardian, keeper of the gates to Grand Hall of the Gods. For a Kirwall warrior, the sight of Rassful meant a life well led, ended in righteous battle, and occurring mere moments after the Val'kyree brought his soul and laid it at the feet of the gatekeeper.

The sights that met my now open eyes did not confirm any of this, however. My gaze was facing downward at the wreckage of my long boat. It was clearly daylight, in an oddly uncharacteristic moment of calm seas and cloudless skies upon the Sea of Ashgul. Debris floated everywhere about as the remains of the hull now lay just below the surface. Realizing I was still lashed to the mast, I mumbled a quick prayer of thankfulness to the gods for sparing me that night.

"Hurry you dogs!" the rough, throaty voice continued barking commands.

Looking up I saw the ship, blacker than a moonless night, and the disheveled sailors upon its deck. Closest to me, several were grabbing anything they thought useful in the water below and pulling it aboard with poles that ended in metal hooks. Two others had yanked the sail rope from the spar and were using it to reach me. Further glances revealed a third group, using long knives to hack away at a black, half-eaten bulk in the water.

"Get it all aboard quickly ere the dragon sharks return for more!" the captain bellowed.

Moving my eyes to take him in brought sudden awareness as to my new circumstances. His loose-fitting clothing covered nearly every inch of his body protecting it from the piercing rays of the sun, but no armor was evident. A wide brimmed hat covered his head, presumably to shield his eyes from the sunlight as well. On one hip he carried a monoscope; the kind Kirwall navigators took on voyages across the sea. On the other was sword unlike the kind land warriors employed. This blade was far thinner and the hilt adorned with a web of metal, presumable to protect the hand of the wielder.

Pirates!

This turn of events was certainly unexpected. Skadiya had taught us about these warriors of the water, clan-less marauders who lived aboard ship and preyed on any craft unfortunate enough to find itself alone on the waves. But, her teachings implied these bandits were lost to antiquity, with no open trade routes between Osherah and the mainland to prey upon once the Yslings began their raids on the clans of the mainland. How they managed to eke out an existence in these modern times was baffling, but not a question I entertained with an immediacy; there were far more pressing matters to discern.

"H-hail Captain!" my voice, strained from thirst and rough with sleep, scratched through the air between us.

"And who might you be," he demanded in response, "that the gods saw fit to give you victory over Leviathan and safe harbor amongst a dragon shark feeding frenzy?" His piercing gaze sought to burrow through my flesh in an effort to unwrap the riddle of my unlikely existence amongst the wreckage of my long boat.

"Clearly you are no accursed Ysling, based on the armor you're wearing – armor I might add that certainly would have dragged you to the deep were you to find yourself without a ship beneath your feet." He surmised, quite accurately. "And, you wield an axe that bears the mark of a Runemaster... Perhaps this is why you yet still live?"

At the mention of mine axe, every sailor amongst them stopped and looked to me, as one they suddenly eyed me a threat.

Clearing my throat and holding my head high I replied in the only manner befitting a warrior. "I am Skarl Kirwall, Runemaster of the Clan Kirwall. Now cut me down you cur and let me aboard!"

Doing his best to hide his reaction from his crew, the Captain's eyes flashed a moment of anger at what he clearly perceived as an insult. But, the flash faded and laughter took its place.

"Hahaha! My what a spirit you possess, Skarl Kirwall!" It was obvious he'd not taken control of this pirate brigade without keeping his wits about him. And, laughing in the face of an obvious insult gave his men license to do the same. I was convinced he saw me as one-part threat, one-part asset, and his next words seemed to prove that suspicion.

"You may be of use to me yet, my waterlogged waif… hurry laddies, get him aboard and bring him something to eat! We sail at next bell!"

+++

"Welcome aboard the *Draugr*, Skarl Kirwall…" the Captain bellowed as I pulled myself to stand on deck. "Runemaster…

"Now, remove that anchor afore it hauls you into the deep."

But, no matter how much he cajoled, I refused to remove my chain mail, despite the captain's instance that were I to go overboard I may as well have a millstone tied around my neck. His name was Edrho, a man I learned was also dubbed 'Red Winter'. According to various members of his crew, he was infamous in the central seas and waterways near Vassa and Hostiveck, both legendary cities of the midlands.

"And just what does a warm water pirate hope to find in the violent, frozen seas where only long boats dare to cross?" My question seemed to sit well with Edrho, as he sat back from the table where we supped, chest puffing out and chin rising in pride.

"A great treasure awaits me in the city of Ashgul and I mean to claim it ere another might beat me to the claim."

Continuing to devour the meat he'd placed before me like a man who hadn't eaten in days, I pushed the topic further. "'Great treasure' you say? And what is so great about it that you risk your very livelihood along with the lives of your crew to sail these deadly waters?" Knowing full well the further north he traveled, the more likely his ship was to encounter a violent storm that churned the seas with ice flows and worse; a storm surge slamming his ship into an ice berg would bring his sojourn to a prompt end. I had to admit that I was developing a growing curiosity as to just what this treasure was.

"It seems the King of Ashgul recently returned from a long journey that led him to Vaasa," Edrho offered, as one might give away knowledge in an effort to gain more. "And, whilst there, the King of Vaasa got a taste for Ashgulian ice spice. Most likely due to its, shall we say, reality-altering properties.

"He soon made it known that he would reward any ship that could bring him a full load of the spice with riches beyond their wildest imaginings," as he paused, Edrho leaned forward, placing both elbows on the table and tilting his head to the side conspiratorially.

"And, my wet friend," his voice lowered, deepened and brought with it an edge I'd not heard thus far. "I plan to be the ship that makes that delivery."

While his plan certainly did not align with my own agenda, it was definitely not mere coincidence that this man, this pirate, happened upon the wreckage of my longboat, out in the middle of the vast Sea of Ashgul.

"That does indeed sound like a worthy pursuit, Captain Edrho," I replied between bites of the last of the Leviathan meat. I examined the final morsel before placing it in my mouth. "Ere now, I'd never tasted the flesh of a monster, unless you count the blood of the ice worm that splattered across my lips when I killed it."

"Ahahha!" the captain let out a mirthful laugh, clearly amused by my lack of fear for him or anything else aboard his ship. "'Ice worm' you say? Never heard of such a creature, but judging by your size and overly-muscled form, I'd wager it a formidable beast. Tell me more, northlander – I find your very existence intriguing."

It was then I heard my opening as he continued "True, I find it hard to believe we merely stumbled across you in a moment of calm waters in notoriously rough seas. No, our meeting was more than coincidence – it was fated by the gods!"

This admittance from him was the proof I needed that he looked favorably upon me as more than a potential curiosity or prisoner or... worse. "I need you to drop me in the waters at the mouth of the Osherah River."

By now, he'd grown accustomed to my directness, and said as much. "Not one for mincing words, are you, my friend? I like that." The smile on his lips widened as his brow lowered, narrowing his eyes. "There are far too many 'civilized' men who fall in love with their own voices, spewing words as if they buy them in bulk and seek to impress the lot of us with their generous usage. Regardless, I need to know, what's in it for me? I've already saved your life, a debt I'm eager to learn how you will repay. I've cleaned you up, fed you a feast and yet still you want more..."

While the vision of Lacina was ever-present in my mind, I held my tongue in regards to my true impetus. "I too, have a debt to see paid, a debt the Yslings must remand in blood. And, let's face it I slayed the Leviathan, you merely came along to enjoy the spoils of my battle with the mighty sea ghost."

"Ha! From the mighty Leviathan, to a school of insatiable dragon sharks, giant ice worms and now an entire country? Is there nothing you fear?"

Remembrances of my dreams, where Lacina remained beyond my grasp, no matter how hard I willed myself forward, flitted through my mind before I answered.

"The loss of my Clan. I am the only warrior of Kirwall this side of The Grand Hall of the Gods thanks to the Yslings and I mean to force a reckoning."

Edrho leaned back in his chair and glanced down at the table pausing briefly before lifting himself to stand. He turned to exit the cabin we dined in, clapping his left hand upon my right shoulder as he passed.

"Let me consider that, Skarl of the clan Kirwall. For now, get some rest." He motioned toward the bunk against the outside wall.

As he exited the room, my mind began replaying the events of the last day. How far had the Yslings managed to sail away from my position? How much farther could Lacina be from me this very moment? What horror was she enduring at the hands of Tristan? As I moved to the bunk and lay my head down, these thoughts transitioned from waking to sleeping nightmares dueling within my mind.

+++

The turbulent waters and storm winds had returned the following morn as we stood upon the deck, staring off towards the horizon.

"I'll repeat my question of yesterday," Edrho turned his gaze upon me. "What's in it for me?"

"There is great plunder among the Yslings," I replied without hesitation, having prepared myself to provide the answer already. "In fact, more plunder than this ship could possible hope to carry."

"And, just how might we, a humble crew of sailing men on a mission to ferry cargo from the great north back to Vaasa, jewel of the Midlands, secure such loot?"

A slight smirk curled the left side of my mouth at his words. "'Humble crew'? It seems you pay too little credit where it's due, Captain Edrho – or shall I call you *Red Winter*?"

Now it was his turn to smile wryly.

"Certainly, a man such as yourself," I continued before he could voice his reaction. "One who earned such a name, could boast of formidable opponents bested and glorious rewards gained in battle."

"That was a long time ago, my friend," he replied as he turned his back to the rail and walked across the deck towards the main mast. "A long time indeed…"

"Well, perhaps the hour is upon us to renew your right to claim such an honorable title, then…" I continued my attempt at persuasion, despite his apparent waning interest.

"And, how might that be done?"

"Come with me, to your cabin where you keep the navigation charts and I'll show you…"

+++

The mid-day sun struggled in vain to shine through the roiling clouds over the violent waves of the Sea of Ashgul. While I felt some sense of relief knowing I was once again in pursuit of the Ysling war party that kidnapped my fair Lacina, I was also fully aware they'd gained at least a day's travel on us. It had taken a fair amount of convincing, but I'd finally persuaded Edrho to take a detour from his journey to Ashgul in search of the mystical ice spice and provide me safe passage to the rocky soil where the Osherah River met the sea. From there, I would travel inland to Osherah itself and gain Lacina's freedom. The memory of her beauty filled my mind, my nostrils flaring at the memory of her scent - a combination of the blue hyacinth that covered the highlands in the months after the spring thaw, and something far more intoxicating.

While we were still a few days sail from the Isle of Azehak where the Ysling town of Osherah lay coiled like the vile serpent's nest it was, I found myself staring intently in the direction we headed, due west, as if I might somehow supernaturally ascertain the exact whereabouts of my Lacina. While the incessant cold wind came raging off the waters for miles around and raped the deck of the *Draugr*, all but the stoutest of Edrho's crew sought shelter below decks. I, however, found the chill invigorating.

"The icy blast reminds me I'm alive!" Edrho announced as he came alongside me to stare at the horizon ahead.

"To many men in the civilized places, towns and great cities, waste their lives chasing after daily comfort and safety. And, for what?" His raised his voice even louder with the question, as if speaking to the gods themselves. "There is no winning against death. It comes for every man sooner or later. No, before I give my last breath away, I want to be assured each one before it had meaning."

"That is… profound," I responded in a lowered tone, not seeing the need to announce my thoughts to the wind and waves as he had. "Particularly for a pirate captain."

"Better to die in pursuit of a great life," he continued, "then to live being pursued by the fear of death."

Turning to lock eyes with him, I couldn't help but ask, "And what exactly does a man dubbed 'Red Winter' live for?"

Clapping his hand on my shoulder, in what I'd come to realize was an indication of his favor, Edrho guided me from the rail and began walking towards his cabin. "I see you will not be satisfied with your time aboard the *Draugr* unless you divine the very origins of all her mysteries, my friend. Come, let's return to my cabin, have something to eat, something to drink, and I may very well regale you with tales of my youth, the ghosts of my past and the specter of my future."

+++

As we sat inside his quarters, dining on more of the Leviathan meat and downing some strange drink Edrho called 'gut-rot', he seemed reluctant to open up about his past at first. After trying it, I found the drink strangely similar to the mead we drank when celebrating in the Great House. Yet, this was less flavorful and left behind a strange burning sensation with each swallow. However, after several glasses of the amber colored drink, Edrho seemed to feel perfectly comfortable sharing the exploits of his past with me, and so much more.

CHAPTER TWELVE: *RED WINTER*

"I wasn't always the captain of this fine ship," he began as his eyes seemed to stare backwards through time. "As a matter of fact, I wasn't always a pirate, believe it or not. I was not much younger than you when the gods sent me on a new path, one I'd never before imagined.

"My parents were wealthy members of aristocracy in Tyras, a mighty city several weeks caravan ride east of Vaasa. The journey was arduous, rising through the southern Nir Mountain range as it splits the mid-continent in half like the spines on a reptile's back. Mother wanted to keep me nearby as always... looking back, it seems having me there always brought comfort to her somehow, as if by focusing her attention on me she needn't acknowledge whatever else it was that robbed her of joy. Father, on the other hand, was determined to make me 'worldly' as he used to say. Convinced I would grow soft sitting around, pampered by my mother, enjoying the fruits of his labor. And, as soon as I was old enough, he sent me off to Vaasa to work in his trading company. It would seem he had quite the fleet of ships at Tyras but was trying to establish a foothold in the port of Vaasa to claim even more territory for his growing trade empire. I recall saying goodbye to mother, as she fought to hold back tears. She seemed as if someone was tearing her heart out... which seemed strange to me at the time. Often when thinking about her, I wonder what haunted her so. In my oblivious, youthful way, I smiled and assured her I would return soon, then begged her not to cry.

"Her final words vexed me for some time. She simply looked up, tears trickling down her cheeks and "goodbye my son, always know that I love you." Perhaps it wasn't actually what she said, so much as how she said it that puzzled me. She seemed as if she somehow knew we would never meet again...

"Upon our arrival in Vaasa, I went about learning all I could about father's business..." his voice trailed off for a moment, as if pondering some lifelong regret.

"If only I had been more mindful of those around me. Instead I simply assumed they would honor my father's wishes and do as they should, while I rose up to lead them. Oh, how naïve I was. In retrospect it was there all along. The jealousy... the indignation... the... betrayal."

"I don't understand..." my words interrupted his reverie and brought focus back to his eyes.

"These men into whose care father had placed me had aspirations of their own. I would later discover they plotted to subvert my father and take the business for themselves. I was a fly in their ointment. A nuisance they plotted to rid themselves of at the first opportunity.

"And that opportunity came in the form of a new contract, trading with a village on one of the islands at the southern edge of the Sea of Ashgul named Valavostia. What a fool I was – but how was I to know the hearts of these men? I'd learned nothing other than hiding behind mother's skirts and clinging fiercely to father's side up until then. While I realize now I couldn't have known better, would that I could have...

"Trusting that the voyage had father's blessing we set sail aboard the *Windlash* at the end of the autumn months. Any seasoned sailor knows better than to take a month-long voyage into the Sea of Ashgul in the beginning of winter, but I was as wet behind the ears as a newborn pup when it came to sailing anywhere other than the tranquil waters of the Tyras Sea.

"I would later learn from the lips of a dying crewman, the captain's orders were to heave me overboard on the return journey, as far from land as possible. Unfortunately for the captain and his crew, I was the only member of the ship capable of returning at all...

"In the weeks of the journey to Valavostia we encountered a few storms, I learned more about sailing on that sojourn than I had in years upon the decks of my father's ships as a child. While he liked to take me out upon the waters, by the time I was old enough to go, father's ailments prevented him from going more than a few hours from port. So, under some pretense of putting the ship through its paces, he would take us out every month or so and use the opportunity to teach me the rudiments of sailing, navigation and what other tidbits of wisdom he felt compelled to share. While he tirelessly taught me other things while at home, sword play, strategy, negotiations and how to deal with lesser men in business, I soon discovered my naval education was woefully lacking.

"But the decks of the *Windlash* were a far more demanding classroom. While most of the crew, as well as the captain, treated me like a slave, there was one older mate who had served with my father in wartime. His name was Ishak, and he took me under his wing – well, at least as much as he could without incurring the wrath of the rest of the crew. On some days, depending on the fickle desires of the captain, I would go without meals. But, Ishak would find ways to sneak fruit or pieces of dried meat to me when no one was looking. Later during the journey, he let slip of losing his own son some years before, a boy just a few seasons younger than me."

Edrho paused for a moment, eyes almost seeming to mist over as a dark shroud obscured his expression. His voice then sunk to a barely audible whisper. "Would that I could have saved you, old man..."

"I'll never forget that morning," taking a deep breath before continuing, the Captain seemed to pull himself from one emotional memory to another, his expression sliding between sadness and anger. "We glided into the cay where our map told us we'd find the villagers. The snow had been near relentless for days, covering the decks with white in every possible shade. It melted in some places, from the warmth below decks, then the relentless winds froze it again all over the *Windlash*. By the time we dropped anchor, the ship seemed as if it was carved from one massive block of ice.

"A lone boat, not unlike the long boats you north men use, but wider and with a cabin amidships, sailed into view and slowly approached us. On the bow stood one man, wearing chainmail similar to yours but with different markings upon the shoulder plates and what appeared to be a white bear skin slung about his shoulders. He was armed with a broad sword that seemed excessively large. At once, he was the most visually powerful and terror-inducing figure I'd seen in my, as then, short life. His arms the size of sail booms, his chest like a keg of ale, and the crooked smile on his face was far more menacing than mirthful.

"There he stood upon the bow, eyes unblinking, staring right through us. This vision of the lone man on the moving ship mesmerized the captain and the entire crew. Never before had anyone seen such a thing and, quite honestly, I'm unsure if anyone knew exactly how to react.

"Just as they were coming alongside, the captain finally found his voice and hailed the warrior of Valavostia, welcoming him and beckoning him aboard. Looking back, I can see the genius in their strategy, and the tragic mistake made by the captain of giving up the high ground. But, how was he to know what was about to occur?

"One by one, a dozen men or more exited the other ship's cabin, each nearly the visually violent equal of the one who stood upon the bow. And, one by one they boarded the *Windlash*, followed by the bowman, who stood upon our deck last.

"'I bring you greetings from Vaa-' was all the captain managed to get out before the bowman's sudden swing cut his head in half just below the nose. There was little time to react to this unexpected turn of events. Before the captain's lifeless body hit the deck, they were among us, dispatching several members of the crew before the other half could draw their swords and defend themselves. We outnumbered them nearly three to one, but they fought with a ferocity our crew had never seen before.

"Ishak grabbed me as I stood there like some fool, mouth agape and eyes wide, pushing me towards the rigging. 'Climb boy, *climb!*' he insisted. And climb I did, not looking back down until I was atop the mainsail.

"It was then I saw the true mettle of some of the men I'd spent the last month sailing alongside. While most were mean of spirit, that character flaw served them well as they fought upon the slippery deck of the frozen *Windlash*. After what seemed an eternity, there were only a handful of men from each side left amidst the blood bath of broken bodies. Among those still living was Ishak who had managed to escape the fighting until the numbers had thinned to a handful.

"Within moments, only two of the enemy warriors remained, and all of our crew had joined the captain in the afterlife, with the exception of old Ishak. Blood was everywhere, covering nearly everything and an almost surreal crimson fog rose from where the warm lifeforce of the fallen was melting the ice that had gripped the surface of the entire ship. Poor Ishak was on his backside, pushing himself away from the two warriors who toyed with him the way a wild dog nips at their prey.

"It was at that instant that something came alive inside me, something animalistic, something insatiable, something… primal… no, evil? I don't know for sure…" his voice trailed off once again. "But, whatever it was, it'd had enough."

"Drawing my sword, I strained to let out a battle cry that never left my lips. Jumping to the deck I swung my sword with all the impetus I could muster from the leap down from on high. Striking one of the warriors in the crook where left shoulder met neck, my blade sunk nearly to his gullet, finishing him in a spray of blood.

"I kicked outward with my right foot into the back of the now dead warrior, while pulling back on my blade to free it from his corpse. The surprise of my attack startled the other warrior who shot his blade forward, piercing Ishak's chest the length of my hand or more.

"It was then I found my voice, screaming in rage as I swung my sword with all that was in me, removing the final warriors head from his shoulders. Looking around in a moment of feral panic, I quickly ascertained no enemies remained. In fact, Ishak and I were all that still drew breath upon the *Windlash's* scarlet painted deck.

"Time seemed to slow then, as the rushing in my ears subsided and I lost my grip on the sword I'd used to dispatch the final two warriors. Rushing to Ishak in hopes of saving him from the icy grip of death, I watched as the light slowly faded from his eyes.

"He raised a trembling hand to cup the side of my face and, through blood speckled lips, uttered those fateful words: 'Th-they bade us to throw you overboard as soon as we cleared land on the return voyage. Oh, the irony that you will be the only one left alive.'"

Carried on a voice barely more than a broken whisper, he breathed his last words. 'I see him… I-I s-see my s-son…'"

"And then he was gone, leaving me all alone on the *Windlash*."

"That's quite a tale, Captain," I said after silence hung in the air until it threatened an awkwardness I was wholly unaccustomed to, since in my culture we celebrated the dead's ascension to The Grand Hall of the Gods where they would feast until the final battle. No, mourning their departure from this world was strange indeed. "But, it still doesn't explain how you became known as the legendary pirate *Red Winter*..."

"Ah, yes, there's that," he continued as his fingers danced across the now empty glass he'd been liberally drinking from throughout his tale.

"After Ishak's death, once the nervous energy of my first true battle wore off, I must have fallen into some sort of shock, or descended into animalistic instinct, for I have no recollection of what happened immediately thereafter. My next memory is awaking in a cabin of the pirate known as Grey Wolf. It would seem he and his crew came upon the *Windlash* still covered in frozen blood, limping its way aimlessly through the Sea of Ashgul. They claimed I was attempting to sail the ship on my own, but no one is up to the task of single-handedly sailing a vessel that requires a crew of two score men.

"His crew, seeing me as some sort of ghost from a frozen hell, bathed in blood, commanding a ship adorned with crimson ice and scarlet frost-encrusted corpses, dubbed me 'Red Winter' that day. Like Ishak before, Grey Wolf took me under his wing until such a time as he went to meet his ancestors and I took command of the *Draugr*, upon which we now sail. While I wanted desperately to exact my revenge on the men in my father's employ who sought to send me to my death, Grey Wolf had other things in mind. But those are tales for another time."

CHAPTER THIRTEEN: *VOIVODE*

The following morning Edrho and I stood once more upon the bow, leaned against the rail, but this time the endless Sea of Ashgul wasn't all that met our gaze. Just peaking over the horizon, glistening in the rising sunlight was the rocky coast of the Isle of Azekah, home of the accursed Yslings. Before long we could see the mouth of the Osherah River, up which we would find the town of Osherah and my beloved Lacina.

To what hellish torture she was facing I could but only guess. Was Tristan forcing his advances upon her now that he had access to private quarters within Viggo's Great House? The Chieftain of Osherah would most likely reward Tristan handily for the destruction of Clan Kirwall. Whilst they had always outnumbered us, they'd been so far incapable of bringing a large enough force to bear upon our shores to defeat us. And, our destruction was something Viggo lusted for since he first learned of our existence. With aspirations of turning the small town of Osherah and

"..I-I...SEE MY SON..!"

building an empire around it, Viggo wanted the fertile lands of Kirwall for his burgeoning kingdom, regardless of whether those lands belonged to us or not.

Or, perhaps Tristan had given up trying to possess the heart of my Lacina, finally accepting the fact that she would never give it to him willingly. And, what is love if it is forced? Nothing at all, I think. No, he would never gain that from her beating heart, which might enrage him further. Would he hand her over to Viggo? Would the Ysling Chieftain take her for his own? I'd never heard of him having a queen to rule by his side, but stories of Viggo were more half-spoken tales and barely remembered myths, since we Kirwalls had no interest in him or his accursed kingdom.

"The sea speaks, you know," Edrho interjected into my reverie, as if he could read my very thoughts. "It spins yarns of human sacrifice and unholy gods worshipped within Osherah. The waves and winds tell of some horror beyond imagining called 'the world serpent-'"

"Ysfang," I interjected. It was not to be expected that Edrho would know of northern gods, for who knew what deities the people of Tyras worshipped? "Born before the world was new, the serpent preys upon those who fall from the favor of the gods, devouring entire nations."

"I've heard the Yslings make sacrifices to this 'world serpent' every full moon," Edrho added. "If they mean to offer up your Lacina, that is, if they haven't already ended her life by some other means, the next opportunity is only a handful of days ahead."

My jaw tightened at the very thought of my Lacina, lashed by each wrist between two Osherah columns, as the demon-god rose up to strike her down.

"Then we must hurry, Captain, as long as a heart still beats within me, no Ysling, snake or demon will escape my furry for placing this indignation upon Lacina."

"Indeed," Edrho responded in an uncharacteristically concise manner.

We both starred out to the shoreline once more, listening to the waves lap against the bow of the *Draugr* as she cut through the waters under full sail.

"Captain!" a voice from on high bellowed, shaking us from our thoughts. "Black sails off the starboard side!"

Turning as one, Edrho and I both spotted the ship, nearly twice the size of the *Draugr* bearing down on us from halfway between us and the horizon.

"Voivode!" Edrho muttered.

Completely unfamiliar with this word, my expression told Edrho as much.

"Raiders of the worst sort. No one knows from whence they hail as so very few live to tell of their encounters with them. The stories I've heard tell of berserker rage, inhuman violence and a rather nasty habit of chopping their enemy's dead into pieces to stir up the dragon sharks before tossing the prisoners they kept alive into the water to watch them die in a feeding frenzy. Their reputation, such that it is, would have you believe they enjoy the destruction of any they encounter far more than what plunder they gain.

"I'm afraid we'll have no choice but to run from them, my friend. As much as I want to help you regain your Lacina, I cannot sacrifice the lives of all aboard the *Draugr* to do so.

"You can either stay on and help us fight them off should they manage to catch us – the gods certainly know we could use a man of your skill and ferocity in such a fight. Otherwise you can jump overboard and swim to land, hoping the currents don't drag you back out to sea..."

Casting my eyes to the water below, it was clear to see the tide was indeed heading outward. With the Island so far away – further still than the *Voivode* ship, the realization that I would not make the swim sunk in. "What's your plan?" I asked Edrho, drawing my axe from its resting place on my belt.

+++

The *Draugr* was tacking to starboard, sliding into the leeward side of the smallish isle closest to Osherah in the boundary island chain that marked the southern edge of the Sea of Ashgul. Stretching as far from the east to the west, the chain was home to hundreds of islands of all shapes and sizes, including the fabled Valavostia from Edrho's tale of his christening with the name Red Winter. Looking over the rail I spied our pursuers, who had gained considerable distance on us. We could now see the host of black garbed warriors on its deck and hear the sounds of their swords as they banged them against shield, rail and anything else within reach in a rhythmic beat that echoed eerily over the waves. The thunderous sound most likely drove fear into the hearts of lesser men.

"C-Captain – a-are we sure we want to tangle with them?" the *Draugr*'s helmsman mouthed the very fear I suspected the *Voivode* hoped to achieve. "Th-they outnumber us three to one..."

"Men!" Edrho bellowed in reply to the helmsman, but loudly enough to address the entire crew. "Legends tell of a race of demons who take human form. They sail from the darkest horizons, seeking to destroy everyone they encounter with agonizing torture and pain. In fact, very few who have encountered these hell spawn have ever lived to tell the tale."

Spinning on his heal to face the center of the ship, he continued. "In fact, I've heard they can devour men's very souls with nothing more than a piercing look from their evil eyes!"

Pausing for a moment to let his words sink in, he looked from one face to the next before speaking again. "Perhaps, they're chewing on your heart right now, Helmsman! Gnawing at the intestinal fortitude that makes you worthy of steering such a great ship as the *Draugr*!"

With that, all eyes turned to the Helmsman, who seemed to shrink back a bit at the accusation. His gaze hit the deck and his shoulders slumped with it.

"Maybe, just maybe, they can swallow us whole from a distance, bringing an end to your wretched life from afar. Do you feel it? Do you feel that pain in your gut? The fear gnawing at your bones?"

Again, silence hung in the air, accompanied only by the sound of wind, wave and the far off pounding from the *Voivode*.

With a sudden outburst that made more than one crew member flinch, the man known as Red Winter let out a deep belly laugh that shattered the silence. "HAHAHAHA! How ridiculous!"

"These are just men, flesh and bone like you and I. They're no more demon than you are Leviathan! Now, put away your doubt! Control your fear! Take hold of your manhood and prepare to fight, dogs!"

As one the entire crew raised their swords to the sky and let out a battle cry that was surely heard on the deck of the *Voivode* ship. Seconds later we slid fully behind the smallish isle, blocking them from our view – and us from theirs.

"NOW men!" Edrho yelled.

In one synchronized effort, the helmsman spun the ship's wheel hard to starboard while several crew members forced the main boom to shuttle across the deck, placing the full sail dead into the northern bound wind. The *Draugr* seemed to leap out of the water, increasing in speed so rapidly, for the briefest of instants, I almost believed I was aboard a Kirwall long boat.

"The *Draugr* is no ordinary galleon, my friend," Edrho offered in answer to a question I had not asked. "Her hull planks are overlaid one upon another, much the same manner as the ships your people and the Yslings use. With the right amount of wind and sail, she raises from the sea and glides across the surface like a water bug. Few craft can match her speed in the right conditions."

As if to prove his point, we were closing on a small bay on the south side of the isle at a pace I'd never expected from a ship as large as this one. Before the *Voivode* could clear the eastern most edge of the isle and regain a sightline on us, we were in the bay and slowing rapidly.

"Drop the sail now!" Edrho bellowed to the crew amidships, before turning to those on the stern. "Lower the anchors, dogs!"

"Now, over the side with you!" he commanded. As one the entire crew with the exception of Edrho, myself and five of his best fighters, leapt overboard. Just as they had jumped into the waters between the land and the ship, the *Voivode* came back into view. As we'd planned, the *Draugr* blocked the overboard crewmen from the enemy's sight.

"I sure hope this works, Runemaster. If not, you'll have to pay me back in hell…" Edrho's words brought a wry smile to my face as my fingers tightened on the haft of my axe.

+++

Their ship, blacker than anything I'd ever seen from hull to mast, sails to rigging, was bearing down on us at a speed that seemed to indicate they intended to ram us. While it was hard to fathom how they'd ensure their own craft would stay afloat upon impact, the wide beamed prow, adorned with a figurehead of stygian demon carved from some naval captain's worst nightmare, seemed intent on crashing into the *Draugr*.

Upon her bow, hanging from one side and the other of the demon headed prow, sailors leaned outward, waving their swords this way and that like a hungry wolf licking its chops at the scent of fresh meat. It was unclear how many were upon the deck of the nightmare bearing down on us, but so far I'd estimated at least thirty fighting men. While the *Draugr* carried a crew of twenty-four, with myself and Edrho added to that, not only were we outnumbered, but based on the appearance of these men clamoring for our blood, one of them was worth any two of Edrho's crew.

"Brace for impact, laddies," Edrho's words barely rose above a whisper as even he seemed in awe at the *Voivode* vessel.

Just as a collision seemed unavoidable, they turned hard to starboard and dropped their mainsails in an almost identical maneuver to the one we'd just performed. However, they left enough sail in the air to still maneuver and kept their anchors aboard. This sudden move had them flanking us, broadside, giving us our first full glimpse of the *Voivode* crew and their captain.

Nearly a head taller than the next largest crewman, the captain was clearly the most physically imposing figure on their ship. This made sense after Edrho's description of their violent lifestyle. Not only did the strong survive, the strongest thrived in their culture. And this captain was a prime example.

His face was masked with a carving of a death's head (or perhaps it was a real skull taken from the carcass of some fantastic beast?), with fangs not unlike those of the snow lions who called the Nir mountains home. The mask covered all but his mouth, which was infested with blackened teeth, each filed to a dagger-like point. His shoulders, almost twice as broad as any of Edrho's crewmen, were equally adorned with skulls, turned sideways with hollow eye sockets staring off to his left and his right. His chest, like two kegs of ale strapped together, was bare showing his highly defined musculature. About his waist hung several more skulls, these clearly human with various indications of the wounds the previous owners had died from upon each one. Gripped in his right hand, a sword unlike any I'd ever seen before. The end of the blade did not come to a point, but angled downward in a hook like manner. I'd later learn the purpose of this design was to rip the flesh from anyone unfortunate to feel the weight of the sword dig into their body.

We locked eyes for the briefest of instants before an evil smile, more wicked than anything I'd ever seen before that day, curled the edges of his mouth up, making him appear all the more sinister. While I'd never truly felt the embrace of fear, it was in that instant I came to understand how lesser men might cower before such a one as this; he seemed more force of nature than flesh and blood human. As these thoughts raced through my mind, my hands untightened and retightened their grip on my axe in anticipation of what was to come.

Raising the mighty blade to my lips, I uttered the spell of the berserker, which was interrupted midway-

"VVVOOOIIIIVVVOOOODDDDEEEEE!"

The captain's war cry ignited an eruption of motion from his crew, some leaping bodily and others swinging from their ships rigging onto the deck of the *Draugr*, as if to overwhelm us in a tidal wave of blackened flesh and blood-stained steel.

Edrho and his men and I were able to make short work of the first wave. I danced between them, dealing death upon any enemy careless enough to come within axe reach. However, the second wave pushed in behind the first, followed rapidly by a third and before long, two of Edrho's fighting men lay among the dead raiders, lifeless. A moment later two more went down, then the fifth.

However, by now I'd taken quite the toll on the enemy crew, drawing the attention of their captain. Grabbing one of the remaining lines, he swung aboard the *Draugr*, knocking several of his own men aside as he landed and swung a blow meant to part my head from my shoulders. He hadn't properly gauged the speed and dexterity possessed by a Kirwall Runemaster under the influence of a berserker spell, however. Ducking his swing, which traveled past me and ripped right through the torso of one of his own men, I spun around and brought my axe around in a circle, hoping to connect with his knees.

Unfortunately, my blow was impeded by a corpse that lay between us, sending the blade careening upward where it slashed through one of the skulls on his belt. Before either of us could recover, a press of bodies separated us as his crew sought to descend on Edrho, who had retreated to the rear deck and was forcing them to come at him one or two at a time. Surveying the scene, I estimated we were still outnumbered roughly twenty to two. I shot a glance over to the *Voivode* ship which had now moved past our flank, with nothing but a helmsman onboard to steer the craft. A moment later they came: the members of the *Draugr*'s crew who had leapt overboard came climbing back onto the deck from behind the *Voivode* warriors, almost unnoticed. Our plan to have them circle the ship and reboard on the opposite side from which they'd jumped overboard in order to catch the enemy off guard seemed to work brilliantly.

As the first of Edrho's returning men clashed with the *Voivode* fighters, the element of surprise quickly gave way to a bloody battle unlike anything most may ever witness no matter how long they live. As expected, the *Draugr*'s crew were certainly no equal match for the enemy, but the odds were much closer with their return. Pressing the attack, I wove a web of shimmering steel, the blurs of glowing runes upon the axe blade weaving in and out of battle, as I sought to dispatch as many of the enemy as I could as quickly possible.

The two sides ebbed and flowed back and forth for some time, until there were far more dead bodies than living ones upon the deck of the *Draugr*. Hacking my way through two who sought to pin me into the forward cabin's doorway, I spied Edrho and two of his men, engaged with the *Voivode* captain. The monster of a man felled the pirate to Edrho's right in one mighty swoop, then brought his giant blade back around, intending to finish Edrho on the return swing.

Suddenly my vision was blocked by two more blackened warriors, both thrusting at my heart in unison. Employing the haft of my axe, I drove their blades downward into the deck, then jabbed outward with my left fist, which was met with a satisfying crunch as it impacted the face of one warrior. Lifting my blade back up, I felt the edge bite into the other warrior's jaw and rip upward before exiting his forehead sending teeth, flesh and bloodied bone flying skyward.

Wild-eyed, I looked around rapidly for the next warrior when I realized that only three of us still remained alive on the deck of the *Draugr*: myself, Edrho and the *Voivode* captain. The next few seconds seemed to move so slowly I felt as if I might be dreaming. Having replayed that scene in my mind a thousand times or more, I clearly recall feeling as if I was trudging through neck deep snow in vain effort to close the gap between myself and the other men. Alas, no matter how rapidly I sought to move, I was too late.

Clearly exhausted from fighting off so many of the enemy warriors, Edrho held his blade up between himself and the enemy captain, as if that thin piece of blood-stained steel would be enough to stop this tornado of torment that was descending upon him. The *Voivode* slapped Edrho's blade aside as one might swat at a gnat. Then, helpless to intervene, I watched as he brought his blade down from right to left, the angled tip digging into my new friend's left shoulder and ripping through until it exited from Edrho's right hip, tearing flesh, muscle and organs out with it.

As I witnessed my friend's fall under the other captain's blade, something caught my eye from the starboard side of the ship. Turning, in full expectance of spying another enemy warrior coming at me, I was taken off guard somewhat by the sight awaiting me. Before I could fully take it all in, the demonic ebony figurehead of the *Voivode* ship's prow blasted through the starboard rail of the *Draugr*, sending splintered wood flying inward in a violent explosion. The pieces of rail, decking and other debris knocked me from my feet, burying me in a pile of shattered ship.

Before the dust could clear, the enemy craft's helmsman came leaping from over the demon head, sword on high as he clearly sought to send me to my ancestors in one fatal down stroke. My legs and left arm were pinned underneath the debris that had struck me when the *Voivode* rammed us and it was clear I would not have time to regain my feet before the helmsman was upon me.

As I watched his violent arc from the bow of his ship to the deck of ours, his obsidian blade, gripped tightly in both fists, coming down on me in what might surely be a fatal blow, I reacted without thought. With my right hand, I grabbed a rather large piece of the ship's rail that lay atop my downed form and angled its splintered end up at the enemy, in the manner a pikesman may sink a spear into the ground and hold the point upward at an opponent.

Unable to alter his trajectory, and too far committed to his death stroke, the helmsman was unable to avoid the splintered rail. His own battle lust was his undoing! He landed full into the make-shift spear, which shot through his chest, splintering breastbone as it instantly ripped through his spine while exiting his back. The impetus of his body, redirected due to the leverage exacted on it by the rail, angled back upward in a new arc that carried him over my head and into the pile of bodies just beyond mine.

Wasting no time, I freed myself from the wreckage as flames ignited where the ebony ship had rammed the *Draugr*. Acrid smoke filled the air as it seemed the winds and waves held their breath in anticipation of what was to come. Turning my gaze, I saw the *Voivode* captain spitting on the downed form of Edrho – upon seeing this my vision turned red, as if I was staring through some sort of scarlet ice at the scene before me.

My recollection of the next few moments is unclear at best, for I'm certain my mind eschewed thinking for instinctual action. The restrained rage I'd felt at the events of the prior week's events let loose and mixed with the remaining effects of the berserker spell. I leapt across the few yards that separated me from the monster of a man who had just delivered the fatal blow to the *Draugr*'s captain, fully intending to end him in one massive swing.

I remember a battle cry escaping my lips on a voice I'm not entirely sure was my own as I brought my axe down in a blow intended to cleave the *Voivode* beast in twain. Standing with his back to me, he might have never known what hit him. However, my cry gave him just enough warning to move to his right, which led to my blade connecting with his left shoulder instead.

The impetus of my rune covered steel was still enough to slice through the ashen skull adorning shoulder, into his steely muscles and black bones before it came out his side, severing his left arm from his body. With reflexes I'd not anticipated from a man of his size, he spun around to his right and brought the hilt of his sword up, catching me in the side of my head which sent me reeling to my left. I recall exchanging a few more swings with the monster, before the blood loss slowed him just enough for my axe to shoot over his guard. In one arcing swing from left to right, I decapitated him, sending his skull adorned head sailing overboard.

I quickly wheeled around, fully expectant of another nightmare to rise up and try to end my life. Except nothing greeted my sight but the eerie silence of a battle field littered with corpses and little else.

Upon realizing I was the only man who remained standing, I quickly turned to Edrho, who lay in a heap, cradling his loosed entrails in a vain effort to prevent them from escaping his body. Kneeling down next to my dying friend, I lifted his head and placed a chunk of clothing torn from one of his dead crewmen behind it to allow him some last moment of comfort.

"D-do they tell tales of days such as this in your Great House, R-runemmaster…" his words came on ragged gasps as blood filled saliva trickled from the edges of his mouth.

"They do indeed, Edrho. You took great account of yourself this day. The gods are certainly pleased."

"G-good. N-now, g-go… f-find your La… La… cin… aahhhh…"

+++

Renewed with what food I could find aboard the *Draugr*, I lowered one of the two landing skiffs into the water, loaded it with the few supplies I could fit and then set about taking care of the dead. Flames from the spilled lamp oils were licking at the deck voraciously and both the pirate ship and the *Voivode* craft were taking on water from their violent impact. Once I'd laid out all of Edrho's crew, I went quickly below decks, wading through rising waist deep water to locate flint and steel as well as an unspilled cask of oil.

By sunset I was rowing away from the *Draugr* as all-consuming flames leapt skyward from its broad deck. Even though Edrho was not a Kirwall by birth, perhaps this grand funeral pyre might catch the eye of the gods and elicit the Val'kyree to take him to the Grand Hall of the Gods where he could regale Runolf, Father and the rest of my clan with tales of the mighty victory we snatched from the feared *Voivode* this day.

Lifting the small mast into place, I raised the sail and aimed the skiff back in the direction we'd come from, while not as fast as the *Draugr*, the small boat should still have me back to the mouth of the Osherah river by morning.

Turning back one last time to spy the flaming wreckage of the *Draugr* which was no longer a feared pirate vessel, but now a final resting place for her courageous captain and crew. I nodded in their direction before lifting my gaze to the dark, roiling clouds overhead.

"Perhaps we shall meet again, my friend…"

CHAPTER FOURTEEN: *LANDFALL*

I thanked the gods for my uneventful journey from the *Draugr's* remains back to the mouth of the Osherah river, where it entered the accursed Isle of Azekah, home of the hated Yslings. By now, I was certain the war party had made their way home and my beloved Lacina was imprisoned in one of their dank dungeons, or worse. While I'd never set foot on the Isle before now, Father had maps and navigational charts he'd insisted I memorize so I might always find my way in the world.

If I remembered correctly, the town of Osherah was a mere few hours up the river by boat, or two days trudge across the rocky earth. Assuming they would have sentries posted along the waters, I spied both shores, looking for a place to stash the skiff should Lacina and I need it to make good our escape. Spotting what appeared to be the entrance of a small cave a short distance upriver, I steered the boat toward it. Finishing up my morning meal in an effort to replenish what strength I might, I put what I would take with me back inside the pack and prepared to make landfall.

Once I was close enough to shore, I jumped into the icy waters and pulled the boat onto the hard ground which was a mixture of jagged black rocks and obsidian soil, and into the cave. Wasting no time, I lashed the boat off on an outcropping of stone that jutted upward into the cave mouth, then grabbed my pack, long knife and axe in preparation of the next leg of my journey. For a moment, I considered the depths of the cavern, which seemed to go on much farther than my gaze could pierce in looking through the shadows that began not far from the entrance. Perhaps they were like the caverns of the Nir Mountains? But, even if they were, having never navigated them before, it seemed a fool's errand to take that way as getting lost in the darkness was an almost certainty. Not to mention the inevitable meeting with whatever horrors called these caves home.

No, I would move along the shoreline, avoiding sentries and traveling as fast as my now exhausted, sleep deprived body would carry me. Taking one last look at the skiff to ensure myself it was properly tied off, I exited the cave entrance and worked my way along the shore, staying just far enough inland to avoid the view of anyone upon the waters, but close enough so as not to lose my way.

+++

The shoreline following the river mouth was comprised of ebon rocks, obsidian soil, half-melted snow, black ice and the occasional tree or shrubbery. After a half hours walk, the path I was blazing forced me to choose to stay close to the water – closer than I desired – or move upward along a ridge of dark rock that rose up to form a cliff that was nearly five times my height at its peak. Choosing the latter, I trudged upward until I found myself walking along a ridge bordered by a dark forest of sorts. The trees, as they were, barely grew to twice my height. While lacking foliage of any sort, each one had a plethora of branches and each of those bore numerous offshoots until the density of trees was thick enough that my gaze could penetrate no further into the forest than several paces would carry me.

Thankfully, the trees stopped roughly the length of a long boat from the edge, as if some invisible line prevented anything from growing so close to the edge. While I quickly became cognizant of the idea that my blond hair, silver chain mail and tan leatherings made my form stand out against the backdrop of blackened branches to any who might spy me from afar, I had no other choice but to keep moving.

I continued on until the sunlight began to wane. Once it fell below the horizon, my heart rejoiced at another sight: an orange glow that shown in the distance. While it was still too far to fully see, I knew this was the glow of torches and fires from Osherah. However, the further I trudged, the darker the night sky became. Try as I might, I could spy no moon casting a glow through the cloud cover and before long I realized continuing on might certainly lead to a misstep that would either tumble me from the cliff face to the jagged ground below, or see me twist an ankle upon some rock I could not see.

Never had I experienced this sort of darkness in the outdoors. A wry smile lifted the end of my mouth as I entertained the thought that such gloom was befitting the home of the cursed Yslings. Finding a spot just far enough into the trees to provide some solace from the icy wind, I cast about to gather as many downed branches as possible in order to build something of a makeshift shelter. I dared not make a fire, lest my enemies see it and raise the alarm. But, the night would only grow colder as the winds from the Sea of Ashgul funneled up the river, intensified in strength by the mouth of the river and my high place above the waters. Sitting out in frozen winds, allowing them to batter me without obstruction would rob my strength even further.

After a short time, I'd gathered enough wooded debris to make a small domicile of sorts by weaving the branches between several trees that bordered the small opening. Placing more upon the ground to fashion a makeshift bed, which would keep the icy rock beneath from leeching the warmth from my body, I took a few moments to eat and drink before much needed sleep overtook me.

+++

Black shapes ebbed and flowed through the icy mists that swam before my vision. The formless shapes changing from clawed monsters scratching at my reality into oppressive clouds that sought to drag my soul into the depths of Hel. How was I to fight such things?! Swinging to and fro, my axe slid through them as if I sought to slice the very air itself. It seemed the harder I fought, the heavier I felt – not just physically heavy, as if I was being weighed down, but heavy in spirit, thought and feeling. Tis hard to fully describe this unnatural sensation of dark, soul crushing oppression.

For the briefest of moments, the center of my field of view cleared and she came into focus. The look of defiance set upon her visage made her even more beautiful, but it was clear something threatened her. As if noting she was there in reaction to my own realization, the black forms turned upon Lacina, once again obscuring her from my sight. Instinctively, I raged forward with all the might the gods had placed within me, but to no avail.

Soon, the darkness was full upon me and gone was anything but stygian shadow and hopelessness.

+++

From an early age, Kirwall warriors, both men and shield maidens alike, learn to sleep lightly. One never knew when death would come and none wanted to leave this life while fast asleep. It was through this instinctual rhythm that I was able to arouse from my dark dream – and while I was thankful it ended so abruptly, I quickly realized I moved from a sleeping nightmare to a waking one.

I could more feel their presence than see them. Moving stealthily through the forest all around me, it was hard to determine exactly how many there were, but that I was outnumbered by a great many was a certainty. Whether it was merely my presence, or the scent of my food that drew them, I knew not. However, it was clear they hungered for flesh and meant to come upon me to feast. It was then I was thankful for my makeshift lodging, which would force them to come at me from the river side of the cliff. Hopefully, no more than one or two at a time.

Standing to my feet and lifting my axe, I steeled myself for the coming battle. In an instant, they came onto the path in front of my sleeping spot and for the briefest of moments I could vaguely see their outlines. Two of them stood between myself and the cliff's edge, backs hunched upward as snarls and growls escaped their slathering jaws.

Wasting no time, I whispered a healing spell, which illuminated the runes on the axe blade. The glow was enough to give me full view of the vile beasts, and seeing it reflected back in their glowing slits for eyes was enough to chill the courage of a lesser man. Each one's torso was nearly the size of my own, supported by six legs, two sets in front and one more powerful set in the rear. Their canine heads were dominated by massive jaws filled with several rows of black, jagged teeth, the front ones shaped like needles, while those further back were serrated like a knife used to cut meat. Legends told of the western Helwolves, but until that moment I always thought them more myth than reality.

Knowing there were several more prepared to take their place should these two fail in their mission to bring me down, I kicked out violently into the face of the one closest to me. Thankfully, the force of my foot took the beast off-guard enough that he skittered backward until his hind legs slid off the cliff's edge. While the first scampered with its two sets of front legs to regain its footing on the top of the cliff, I swung my axe full upon the head of the other slicing through it in a sickening explosion of bone and brain.

As expected, the rest were full upon me now, forcing their way between one another in a rabid frenzy of hunger and instinct, seeking the solitary goal of feasting on my flesh. My only salvation was the nature of my shelter which prevented them from descending on me all at once.

I kicked out again at the third, who came from my right, sending him crashing into the first, which propelled them both over the edge. The fourth took that opportunity to leap at me, propelled forward by its mighty hind legs, jaws agape in what was intended to land a killing blow on my throat.

Ducking with all the speed and agility I'd ever known, I was able to dodge the Helwolf, and bring my axe around to slash into his left shoulder, severing the two left forelegs and effectively ending the thing's attack upon me. Wasting no time, I spun around to face the others, slashing and slicing with my axe as rapidly as I could. Before long, we fought in a pile of Helwolf carcasses, making the ground slick with their lifeblood.

I have no recollection of just how long the battle raged but do recall the eerie silent nature of it. Once engaged, the vile beasts no longer growled or seemed to make any other noise. Their blackened shapes simply set upon me one after the next, seeking to drag me down. Just how much longer I could withstand their onslaught, I did not know.

I do, however, clearly recall realizing it was just myself and what I could only assume was the leader of the pack remaining. This one was larger than all that had come before, with a thicker torso, more muscled legs and several jagged scars that criss-crossed its head and face. It was clearly one of the most formidable predators I'd ever seen. Perhaps this thing might even be the equal of a full-grown male snow lion?

We stared at one another as he paced back and forth behind the pile of bodies between us, cunning more than instinctual hunger seemed to lurk behind its obsidian eyes. Acutely aware of the dozen or more cuts I'd endured from the teeth and claws of his packmates, it would seem the beast was emboldened by what it thought was a weakened prey. More than once I noted its nostrils flaring in a manner that exposed the blood-stained upper teeth. The fact that it had no clear path to me due to the carcasses of its packmates worked in my favor, giving a few moments reprieve from battle.

However, I'd based its abilities on my experience fighting the others. Judging a distance I assumed to be too far for this monster to close in one leap, I set my feet and prepared to swing full in front of me where I anticipated it would land. To say this was a mistake is an understatement.

Issuing a roar that shattered the night silence and jolted me with its ferocity, the beast leapt toward me with more power and violence than I'd seen from any of the others. Before I could bring my axe around, the beast hit me full in the chest, sending us both crashing backwards in an explosion of splintered branches and sticks.

Using its momentum, I grabbed a handful of fur about its neck and sought to roll it over me by kicking upward with both legs while pulling my grip downward with all my might. The beast did indeed carry over me at this point, but it's travel was halted abruptly by the trunk of another tree several feet behind the now shattered back wall of my shelter. Before

...PROPELLED FORWARD BY ITS MIGHTY LEGS.

I could regain my feet, it was upon me once more. The obstructions from trees and branches prevented me from bringing my axe to bear on the beast; my shelter, which had been a boon through the battle so far was about to spell my doom.

Slathering jaws ripped at my chain mail as I braced the mighty beast's neck far enough away with my free hand to prevent it from sinking its front teeth into my neck or face. The rancid smell of rotten flesh wedged between its back teeth was full upon its breath, nearly choking me of mine. It's hind-legs jumped from side to side, as the monster sought to further drive into me in some primal desire to end my life once and for all. However, the continual movement prevented it from applying enough constant pressure to achieve its goal; the thing was too eager to kill me and that was all the opening I would need.

+++

SLAP!

The flat of Father's axe caught me full upon the backside, sending me sailing into the snow, face first. "Again!" he yelled at me before I'd completely halted my fall.

Regaining my feet as fast as I could I lifted my wooden sword and charged him once more. At nearly ten winters old, I was almost tall enough to stare Father in the chest, but, despite my recent growth spurt, he was still much larger than I. In my young mind, I was convinced that sheer force of will was my only hope in landing a blow on an opponent as large as him – something I'd yet to do in all our years of mock battling.

As I charged him once more, he again side-stepped my assault, this time reaching out and grabbing the back of my head and shoving hard in the direction I was already traveling. This extra momentum, added to my own, sent me sprawling into the snow face first.

Before I could stand once more, I felt his hand grab me by the shoulder and lift me to my feet. Taking the sword from my hand, he knelt before me and brushed the snow from my clothing and hair. The smile I'd come to know and love played across his face as his eyes saw me fully.

"A fight takes place more in the mind than the body, young Skarl," his powerful, gruff voice was enough to stop a grown warrior in their tracks, but also had a rich quality to it that drew people to him. "You must think your way to victory, without stopping long enough to think your way to defeat."

"What do you mean? I d-don't understand..." as was often the case, Father would need to further explain his battle wisdom before my young mind fully grasped it.

"A warrior who acts without thinking will often place himself at the opponent's mercy, just as you did right now. Upon realizing you were unthinkingly charging at me I was able to use your own momentum against you by first dodging your assault, then adding to your forward momentum to knock you off-balance. I was able to do this by thinking then acting, instead of merely reacting."

"But, how am I to know what to think, what to do?"

"Practice, my son," And with that he tossed my wooden sword upon the snow and raised his axe once more. "Now, go again!"

+++

Remembering Father's words, a cunning smile curled my lips. Waiting for just the right opening, when the beast planted both hindlegs at once in a mighty effort to force its way through my guard with all its strength. In one fluid movement, I rolled to my right, pulling the monster's bulk along with me, propelled forward by the impetus of its own hind legs. The monster crashed into the carcasses of its fallen packmates and before it could regain its footing I was up and upon it.

A flurry of blows descended on its back, neck and head, the final eliciting a snarling yelp of pain from the old beast. For the first time it retreated, backing away from the reach of my blade, which was exactly what I hoped it would do. Leaping forward and issuing a battle cry of my own, the first sound to exit my lips so far, I drove the Helwolf backward until one of its hindlegs slipped over the edge of the cliff, sending a handful of gravel and loose dirt flying down to the river below.

The loss of footing surprised the thing, causing it to react by glancing backward to see where it was standing.

"Never take your eye off your opponent in battle," was another of Father's wise teachings. He'd often have others throw things at my back, attempt to trip me or otherwise create distractions meant to get me to look away from my attacker. This included what seemed like an eternity of blindfolded battle. Thankfully the sire of this old wolf had passed down no such wisdom.

Slashing down in the first full swing I'd been able to achieve as I was now clear of the shelter and surrounding trees, my axe blade sheered into the snout of the Helwolf causing it to retreat further and slide over the edge. After an instant, the wet thud of the beast striking the rocky shore below filled the air, then all fell silent once more.

+++

While I did not feel well rested, it became certain the night had passed with many hours of sleep followed by the battle with the Helwolves. For, no sooner had I pushed all the carcasses over the cliff's edge than the rising sun began to bring light into the darkness. Removing my morning meal from the pack, I devoured it quickly, hoping to make my way to the outskirts of Osherah by nightfall. If all went as planned, today would be the last day my beloved Lacina would suffer the humiliation of Ysling captivity.

Once done with my food, I checked to make sure nothing had fallen from my pack during the previous night's disturbance and continued my journey upriver. As the sun climbed in the sky and reached its peak, I began noticing signs in the ground that I was not the only person to pass this way recently. Kneeling to inspect the first prominent cluster of steps I encountered, it was clear this was but a single person, traveling forward and back again. Judging by the size of the prints and depths they sunk into the ground, it was easy to determine this was either a woman, a child or a smallish man. The to and fro nature of the tracks explained why I'd not seen them further down river; whoever this was came out here for some specific goal before returning from whence they came.

Standing once more I continued my journey. Before long the awareness I was not alone came upon me. Examining my surroundings with peripheral vision, lest my head motions alert my follower to the idea I was aware of their presence, I sought another alcove in the tree line not unlike the one I'd made a bed in last night. As with the wolves, I wanted to force this person to come at me from a direction of my choosing, not theirs.

But, before I found such a place, the choice was taken from me.

CHAPTER FIFTEEN: *PREDATOR OR PREY?*

Standing no taller than I was at ten winters of age, the old woman appeared before me as if from nowhere. At once she began eyeing me up and down, as if spying on me for the last hour wasn't enough and she yearned for a closer inspection. Adorned in a ragged array of cloaks, none of which was without significant rips, tears and holes, she reminded me of the demi-god Rigel. One part waif, one part mischief maker, Rigel tread the world seeking the death of children so he could steal their clothing for his own. As it was mainly a tale told to little ones to scare them into performing their chores, I'd not thought of the demi-god in many winters. But either this woman was trying her best to appear just as Rigel might, or she was truly clothed in the articles scavenged from corpses. However, it was easy to see she had once been quite beautiful, before the ravages of time robbed her of that gift.

"Who might you be?" she uttered in a voice that was half female half nails dragging across rusted metal. We locked eyes briefly before her gaze fell to my axe.

"I am but a weary traveler, my lady," it seemed unwise to divulge my true identity to one so mysterious as this, particularly with less than a day's travel between us and the Ysling city.

"Indeed, weary you do look, of that I'm certain," she continued eyeing me up and down as she went on. Her hands, gnarled from too many years of hard labor, clawed at the air between us. "However, I find nothing 'but' about you. You carry yourself like a seasoned warrior, armed with the tools of that trade. Yet, there is nothing Ysling in your appearance…"

Before I could respond, she turned her back and motioned down the trail in the direction I was headed.

"Come," she more ordered than requested. "This way, 'weary traveler'."

As she turned, she moved ahead at a pace I'd not expected from a woman of clearly advanced age. In fact, I had to quicken my pace to keep up with her, lest she disappear from sight. We moved at our accelerated pace for some time. Knowing we were growing closer to Lacina with every footstep, I was content to follow the old woman for now. However, the notion that she might be leading me into a trap was ever present in my thoughts.

Just as I was noticing the approach of evening, the haggard old woman stopped momentarily, looking this way and that, before darting into the woods. While her smaller form allowed her to move through the tangle of blackened branches far easier than I could, I was thankful to note she didn't travel far off the trail before stopping and kneeling down.

Brushing away a few dead branches, she grabbed hold of an iron ring, hidden from view up til now, and stood back up, using the ring to open a trap door in the forest floor.

"In!" she commanded, nodding her head towards the dark opening below the door.

My fingers tightened on the haft of my axe subconsciously, which was not lost on her prying eyes.

"No need to fret, young warrior. There are no friends of the Yslings in the *down below*."

Something about this woman brought an ease of familiarity, as if we'd met before, even though I knew I'd never set eyes upon her before this day. But, that feeling was enough to entice me to follow her direction. Looking through the trapdoor, I leapt down into the darkness below.

+++

Once my eyes began to adjust to the darkness, I was able to discern we were in some form of tunnel, not unlike those that splintered off the Nir caverns of my homeland. These, however, seemed to be carved through the dirt and rock with tools of human origin. If my sense of direction was accurate, we wound our way towards Osherah, which suited me fine. However, I was growing anxious to determine our progress. As if she could sense this, the old woman broke the eerie silence.

"Not much further, young warrior," she offered, at barely above a whisper. "Almost there, almost there."

It was then I noticed a growing orange light from out ahead of us. With each successive step, we drew closer and closer to the source. Before long, it was easy to assume the light was from torches – many of them if I had to guess. A moment later and we turned into a large, open area, that seemed more like the inside of a Long House than a cave of any kind.

Looking about, I saw bunk beds lining the walls, each with its own unique set of personal effects from fur blankets and packs, to clothing and weapons. Towards the center of the room was a series of tables, each sparsely covered with food and drink. By my quick calculations based on the number of beds and tables, I surmised upwards of fifty people lived here.

Once again, anticipating my question, the old woman spoke before I could. "Welcome to the *Down Below*. Home of the free men and women of Osherah."

"'Free men and women'?" I echoed her statement in the form of a question.

"Yes. Sit, sit, and let me get you something to eat," she grabbed a plate, placed some sort of purple fruit, a few chunks of bread and what appeared to be stag meat on it before setting it down before me. Turning quickly, she grabbed a cup carved from a ram's horn, filled it with mead from a metal pitcher and set that in front of the plate. "Now. Eat."

The feeling as if I was being mothered to some degree brought back thoughts of my own. The memory of her broken body lying behind father's in the ruins of Kirwall brought involuntary anger to my visage, which seemed to alarm the old woman.

"What is it? What troubles you so?" she asked in a soothing tone I'd not heard from her thus far.

Taking a deep breath to regain my composure, I replied. "Painful memories assail my thoughts, visions I cannot put to rest until my mission here is done."

"Yes, yes… I've seen men driven by the lust for revenge before. You don't conceal it well."

"I've no need to hide my heart, woman. But, please continue, I would know what this place is and what you meant of 'free men and women.'"

"Yes, yes of course," she muttered, appearing to hold back a slight disapproval of my response. "The free men and women of Osherah. We all were once free men and women of other lands, but the *Three Fates* destined to bring us here to this accursed place. While we all have our own stories of woe and pain that led to this moment, it is through those journeys, one by one, we found ourselves enslaved by the Yslings.

"Some captured in battle, some stolen from home villages at night, some taken from ships raided by Ysling longboats. We were treated as property… less than dogs… disposable labor. However, many winters ago, myself and a few others discovered the cave entrance that leads here, just outside the walls of Osherah, beside the pond where their sewers empty. At the back of that cave, we discovered a small passageway which we carved out over many seasons until we found this room. Finding the right moments to escape, one by one we did so, after slowly filling this space with supplies stolen bit by bit from our Ysling masters. We were careful to never take enough at any one time for it to be noticed.

"Once we realized they would not come looking, for who goes after a valueless dog that runs away? Our true vision came upon us. We would use these tunnels to take other slaves back to the life of freedom. Now, one by one, each moonless night, we take a slave to the coast and set them free upon the waters, hoping the *Three Fates* will see them safely returned to their homelands."

"Tis a noble cause you've undertaken here, woman. But, what of you?"

I asked gruffly, pausing just long enough between bites of the stag meat I was rapidly devouring and hearty gulps of mead. "Why have *you* not left?"

"I have nothing to go back to…" at this, it was her turn to show her dysphoric emotions upon her brow, reflected in her saddened brown eyes and drawn down upon her lips.

"Nothing? Surely anything is better than this?" I asserted, motioning at the cave around us, wondering why anyone would embrace a life led hiding in the darkness. Before she could reply, I parried with another question. "And, how is it you came to be here in the first place. You hardly seem the type to have fallen in battle, and clearly you don't have northern blood in your veins."

"Mine is a sad tale indeed," she deflected. "Surely a mighty warrior like yourself has no interest in hearing such things."

"Indeed, I do. In my homeland we regale one another with such stories when we dine, in this manner we learn to see one another truly, so we know whose life we might give our own to protect." My admission to defend her with my life seemed to catch her off guard, but for a Kirwall, defending those who showed you kindness came as natural as breathing.

"Alright, if you insist, young warrior. But, before I tell you my sad story, you must tell me your name."

"Skarl. Skarl Kirwall of the clan Kirwall," I grunted between bites of meat.

"Okay, young Skarl," she nodded toward me without breaking eye contact; a behavior I would later learn was a sign of respect in her culture. "We have time, and you've clearly not eaten your fill…"

+++

"As a young woman, I had occasion to marry a very wealthy man, who was several winters older than I was upon the fateful day of our wedding. In me, I believe he simply saw an object of his lust, a young virgin who pleased his eye. In him, I saw a man of great ambition and success. Would that I'd been wise enough then to discern he had no love for me, only carnal desire, I might not have accepted his offer of marriage.

"Before long I was pregnant, and we had a son. While my husband never showed me one ounce of love, our son became my heart. Watching him grow, discover the world around him, play, laugh and mature was the best experience of my bleak existence. Behind closed doors my husband, an easily angered man, took his wrath upon me, beating me often for failed business deals, lost profits and any other lack of success his business endured. It was as if he believed he could exercise his lack of good fortune by physically abusing me.

"However, I endeavored to persevere. If nothing else, I did so for my son. While his father seemed incapable of affection, he did teach him the ways of men and helped him grow into a fine young lad. Then, one day, he sent our son away and once more I was the sole focus of my husband's homelife.

"After one of the more violent assaults he put upon me, I overheard him speaking with one of the men who worked for him. They discussed a matter of betrayal that sent my husband into a rage far greater than I'd ever seen before. Knowing I might not survive another such beating, I slipped out of our home and disappeared into the night.

"With the only light left in my heart kindled by the hope of being reunited with my son, I traveled to the place my husband had sent him. Upon arrival, I found no sign of him. While asking about, I learned that not only had my husband been murdered the very night I left, but our son had been sent on a journey he was not meant to return from by the very men accused of killing his father.

"Taking what little jewelry I had, I used it to book passage on a ship to follow the path my son's journey had taken, in the hopes of saving him, and myself, from this cruel twist of fate.

"But, before our ship arrived at the destination, we were raided by Yslings, where I and a few others were taken as slaves."

A wry smile played across my lips as I titled my head to the side and locked eyes with her. My expression seemed to offend her, but she did her best to hide that from me.

"Why do you smile, young Skarl Kirwall? Does my sadness bring you joy?"

"What is your name, old woman?" ignoring her question, I pronounced one of my own.

"Darla," her expression a mixture of confusion and shame at not having told me her name thus far.

"Your story sounds familiar to me, Darla, your son," I continued. "What was his name?"

"Edrho..."

CHAPTER SIXTEEN: *THE THREE FATES*

Tears made clear trails down her dirty face as I told Darla about the life her son led, and his unfortunate death just a few days before.

"The *Voivode*?" she muttered between stifled sobs. "I've heard speak of them. They might be the only people the Yslings truly fear."

Lowering her head, breaking our eye contact for the first time since we sat down, the reality of her life seemed to fall full upon her, driving her shoulders down with the full weight of her fate. "A mere few days… if only your ship would have come here several days ago, we would have spied you out on the coast. A-and… m-my s-s-son…" her voice trailed off in misery.

Unaccustomed to this sort of expressive grief, I found myself not knowing what to say. "He was a great man, your Edrho. I'd hazard a guess he was the greatest I'd ever encountered outside of mine own clan. I can only hope he feasts with the gods this very night."

Without lifting her gaze from the floor, hands fiddling with the ragged cloaks she wore, the Darla continued her lament. "If only my ship had been sieged by the same pirates who took my Edrho – we would have been reunited many winters past. To wish him goodbye, only to spend the next dozen or more summers looking for him…" her voice trailed off before continuing. "And, to know he died but one day's sail away. Oh, how cruel the Three Fates can be! What a laugh they must have had when they wove my life into the grand tapestry of creation…"

Without thinking, I finally found myself asking, "What are the Three Fates you keep mentioning?"

This question actually brought her head up and we once again locked eyes. "Yes, yes, that's right… you're a Northerner. You worship pagan gods like the Yslings."

"Pagan gods," I repeated, unsure of what this meant.

"Oh, no offense my dear, but the peoples of Njordica acknowledge many different deities. Some even claim there is 'one, true God.' A God who loves His people and craves a relationship with them – how strange does that sound? But, my people know the tapestry of the Three Fates to be true. And, the Three Fates aren't a 'what,' but rather a 'who.' Three identical sisters who spend every moment, day and night, at the eternal loom, weaving the tapestry of all creation. It is they who determine your life – knowing it from birth to death – and leaving us to live it out to discover what they already know: we are all fated to something, no matter what decisions we make, what actions we take, what sort of life we try to live."

My brow furrowed at such a strange concept. I'd always known of the gods, that we were often their playthings, pawns in their games. Yet mighty Adon, king of the gods, cared not about our fate, paying attention only to the degree that we might fill his eternal army. Nothing was set in stone, we were fated to live a life of free will. However, a person who sought to change their destiny could do so by pleasing the gods, most often in battle. The idea that our lives were already laid out for us seemed… stifling, imprisoning, hopeless. Why even live such a life? Surely it was not worthy of a warrior to do so…

The confusion on my face pulled her from her grieving for a moment.

"And, please forgive me, I know your ways are to celebrate the lives of the dead, feeling glad hearted of their invitation to the Grand Hall of the Gods. Such a way of life must save the heart great pain – even if the body endures far more in getting there."

It was then our conversation was interrupted as roughly a dozen people, all but one dressed as rag tag as the old woman, entered the room. Their leader seemed to be a warrior of sorts, or at least was dressed in the clothing one might wear under a warrior's armor. Upon spying me, they took up arms, fearing I was somehow threatening her, as she was clearly in distress. They were but ten paces from us as my instincts took over. In one swift motion I rose from my seat, drew my axe and was just about to leap towards them when her smallish hand grabbed my right arm.

"No Skarl! These are friends," she yelled in alarm. "Jorgen! Stop – this is Skarl. H-he k-knew my son…"

The man at the forefront of the group, Jorgen, made a motion with his free hand towards the ground as he lowered his sword. The other men and women with him did the same.

"What's he doing here?" Jorgen, leader of this band of misfits and would-be warriors, demanded. He stood nearly my height and was clearly a strong man judging from the rippling muscles in his arms, or at least what was visible of them. His hair was dark brown and somewhat curly. His bluish skin reminded me of tales Father had told of people from other cultures he'd met on his youthful adventures. He looked upon me with reserved approval, as if Darla's word would stay his blade, but he was wise enough not to trust me entirely based on her insistence.

"I've come to end the Yslings," the steely tone of my voice seemed to convince them my words rang true, as Jorgen and the others all broke into wry smiles, sheathed their weapons and approached the table with glad tidings.

+++

The following morning, Jorgen and I were on the roads of Osherah. Several winters my senior, he carried himself with a weariness of some-one who had endured too much in too short a time. Despite that, he was the most able-bodied former slave in the *Down Below*. We woke early, put on cloaks and made our way out of the caves and into the sewage pond. Once there, we used the human waste to cover our cloaks with excrement – confused as to the reason for this – and disgusted by the awful scent that assailed my nostrils, I balked at first. "Why must we do this?"

"The Yslings will avoid us at all costs due to the sight," Jorgen offered in reply "and *smell*, of our appearance. For, why would anyone worth a war-rior's respect walk around like this? They will see us as human dung, or worse. This will allow us to roam freely in the common areas. And that is how we will discern the whereabouts of your Lacina."

"And just how do you know all this? The tricks to avoid Yslings, the whereabouts of their prisoners?" I asked, skeptically.

"My former master was of the artisan guild, descended from the origi-nal Ysling families who built Osherah long ago," Jorgen replied. "He kept me about as part physical labor, part body-guard, depending on my strong back to do a great many things for him. And with that familiarity, came reward. Not only have I had the privilege of standing within every building in the town; I've also overheard secrets, seen things, observed behaviors. The Yslings are far too prideful to think a slave might ever know too much, so they never deigned to curb their tongues in my presence."

Satisfied with his reasoning, I continued applying the elements of the ruse. My nose wrinkled with the horrid smell as I secretly hoped Lacina would never learn of this, nor stand downwind of me. The shiver of dis-gust ran through me as I choked back a gag reflex, which was met with a chuckle from Jorgen.

As we walked between the many long houses, I marveled at how much larger their town was than our modest village of Kirwall. Each road we passed was nearly three times longer than any span of Kirwall and their population was far more mixed than ours as well. While the majority of the people were Yslings, there was also a great number of slaves of every creed and culture. A third group made up the smallest minority of the popula-tion: merchants, but they too were a diverse bunch.

"They've begun to let foreigners ply their trades in Osherah recently – for a hefty fee," Jorgen explained. "While the few I've spoken with com-plain about the taxes they pay, they've little choice if they want to sell their wares in this part of the world. And the Yslings lord that over them with contempt and greed."

We moved closer to the center of Osherah. Ahead I saw the road open up into a town square of sorts, complete with a variety of merchant stands, tables and carts upon which sat various food stuffs, tools and other oddities of which I was wholly unfamiliar. At the far end of the square was a large, raised dais cut from some sort of limestone with twin ivory columns on each side. The bejeweled columns reached skyward, taller than the roofline of the Great House of Kirwall and upon each one hung a steel ring and triple braided cord, presumably to restrain the sacrifice. From between the columns and moving toward the back of the dais, the limestone had a crimson tinge to it, most likely from the blood of those devoured by Ysfang in their unholy ceremonies. Behind the dais was more of the obsidian forest I'd traveled through on the way here. The gnarled, black trees made an eerily contrasting backdrop for the white stage.

"Is that it?" I asked Jorgen to verify my suspicions.

"Yes. The altar of sacrifice. Tis where they make offerings to Ysfang, the world serpent."

The hackles on the back of my neck stood on end at the very thought of my Lacina, bound between those columns, awaiting the slithering nightmare that sought to ravage her.

"They say Ysfang was old before the world was new," Jorgen continued. "He wraps his coils around the very fabric of our reality, containing the lands and preventing the seas from spilling into the afterlife. They say there is a delicate balance between his movements and only through living sacrifice are the Yslings able to keep the beast from constricting his body and killing us all."

"I've heard such stories myself, Jorgen. Yet, on some level I always thought them more myth and legend than reality."

"I know not how true the surrounding tale of the creature is," Jorgen added. "However, I've seen the thing with my own eyes as it crushed the life from my bride, Yasmeena..." Pausing to regain his composure before continuing, a pained, far off look crawled across Jorgen's face. "She and I met in captivity and stoked the fires of our romance in secret lest our masters discover and punish us both for our impropriety. We were to be married the very day they took her... I pray to all the gods that we can prevent you from experiencing the same waking nightmare, Skarl Kirwall."

Clapping him on the shoulder, I sought to reassure him. "Then, we shall have your revenge this day, my friend. For, I meant what I said when we first met. No Ysling horror shall stay my hand nor prevent me from gaining Lacina's freedom."

"Would that you had been here for Yasmeena…" It seemed unnatural for another man to voice a desire for someone else to save his family, but the oddities of Jorgen's culture were still a mystery to me. He'd told me of his homeland, Galtek, but it was the first I'd heard of such a place. Father had mentioned men and women such as Jorgen to me, but apparently had never traveled to a place where they might originate. Clearly, the world was much larger than I'd believed it to be just a few short weeks ago.

"This way," Jorgen motioned in a very understated manner so as not to draw attention. We moved across the square, doing our best to avoid the paths of any Ysling warriors. When we first entered the square, I'd counted roughly fifty of them in sight. If Jorgen's words were true, there were hundreds more in the long houses and surrounding streets. As much as I yearned to strike them all down, the wise course of action was to keep our identities a secret. Better to escape notice as filthy slaves, than raise an alarm before my plan was fully realized.

We moved out of the square, down a road between houses that led off to the left of the sacrificial altar. Before long, I noted the number of Yslings increasing and the number of slaves and merchants decreasing.

"Are you sure this is wise?" I whispered, in order to draw as little attention as possible.

"She's down this way," Jorgen replied in a quieted voice of his own I had to strain to hear. "I'm sure of it."

As we passed the long house that made up one side of the road, we came to an intersection where a great many people were thronged together, looking out to the road that was crossing ours. A moment later, I saw two horses with Ysling warriors upon them coming down the other road. Behind them, they pulled a cart and upon the cart was a sight I'd yearned to see for many moons. My heart at once leapt into my throat upon laying eyes on her, then was rapidly washed back down in a wave of crimson rage. Her hands were chained together, her beautiful face downcast in a look that was one part hopelessness, one part defiance. Standing alongside her was the vile Tristan Angivar with a look of pride and satisfaction on his face. Clothed in the armor of a high-ranking Ysling soldier, it would seem the betrayer had finally received the station in life he'd always craved.

On her other side was a tall Ysling warrior I'd not seen before that very moment. Jorgen would later tell me he was Lukas, their Runemaster. Unlike Tristan and Lacina, he wore no emotion on his grey face, seemingly cold and dispassionate, brown eyes staring ahead unblinkingly in the direction they were headed. That he was closer in age to my Father than

"THIS WAY," JORGEN MOTIONED...

myself was evident in the grey flecks throughout his black beard and braids. His frame just as formidable. However, like Father, despite his advanced life, his musculature still rippled under the aging skin and the internal power of an elder Runemaster flickered in his piercing eyes.

"Where are they taking her?" my whispered question was drowned out by the boisterous crowd who were shouting and gesticulating in a mixture of cheers and jeers. Raising my voice a little, I repeated the question.

"My guess is the prison house, it lies just a few roads over," they must be coming from the Great House, which lies back the way they came.

Unknowingly, my right hand had closed on the haft of my axe, which was hidden underneath the awful smelling cloak I wore that day. Thankfully, Jorgen noticed before I removed the axe from my belt and made use of it. He reached down and grabbed my right wrist as we locked eyes. "Not now, my friend, you serve her not in a pointless death."

As the horses and cart moved past the intersection, the crowd filled in behind them allowing us to continue watching. They made their way down to another long house, with multiple Ysling guards standing around it. The cart came to a halt here, and Lukas jumped down motioning to two of the guards to open the doors to the house. Tristan jumped down as well, roughly pulling Lacina with him, before shoving her into the house ahead of him.

At this, my anger took hold as I reached for my axe once more and took a step forward. Thankfully, Jorgen was able to step in front of me and prevent me from acting unthinkingly. "Patience, Skarl, we know she's alive and relatively unharmed. And, most importantly, we know where she is.

"Now, come!" Stepping out from in front of me, Jorgen went back the way we'd come, motioning me to follow.

We moved quickly, whilst everyone's eyes were on Lukas, Tristan and their party. Moving back to the end of the next long house, Jorgen ducked down behind it and we made our way between it and the house beside it. Once through, we turned back in the direction of the prison house. After a moment, we stopped, just out of sight of the guard positioned closest to us.

"Remember what we discussed," Jorgen implored me in a hushed tone. "We need silence and stealth, so perhaps you just keep that axe of yours on your belt for this one."

Peering around the corner from where we hid, I could see the Ysling guard, looking bored senseless by his current lot in life. If he only knew how much more exciting it was to become! I waited for my opportunity and after a moment, he turned his back full upon us. Sliding up behind him, in one rapid movement I stood fully, reached out with my right hand and grabbed the back of his head, while my left grabbed his chin. Before he knew what was happening, I'd spun his head so violently to the left the only sound he was able to make was a muffled gurgle that followed the decisive snap of his neck. The man was dead before his body had a chance to hit the ground.

Jorgen rushed over and we carried the body off and slid him under a nearby long house. Wasting no time, we stripped him of his chainmail and accoutrements, leaving him in his undergarments. Removing my cloak, I quickly donned his armor, then draped the cloak back over myself to hide the guard's uniform from prying eyes. Once done, we carried him back out into the small alleyway between houses and sat him on his rump, propped up against the side of one of the houses between two barrels.

Pulling a flask from his cloak, Jorgen removed the cork and poured the liquid inside into the dead man's mouth and all over his face and clothes. Once he'd drained the flask, he placed it in the man's hand. Then, we were away as quietly as we'd arrived, leaving nothing but what appeared to be an Ysling who had drank himself to death. With any luck, he would not be discovered anytime soon.

Making our way through the maze of alleys between the long houses, we were just entering the sewage pond when we heard quite a commotion behind us. The cacophony began with the scream of some woman, followed by men's shouts and sounds of alarm.

"It would seem they've found our handiwork, young warrior," Jorgen smirked as we descended through the cave entrance and back to the *Down Below*. "Thankfully, the Three Fates wove a victory for us this day."

CHAPTER SEVENTEEN: *A RECKONING*

We sat about the table in the cave where those who still called the *Down Below* home lived. I had secretly hoped to recruit them all to help in my cause, as it was more than apparent there were too many Yslings for one person to overcome alone. But, in looking at them all gathered now, it was clear but a handful of them were actually suited for combat, and of those only Jorgen seemed to come from true fighting stock. Several were hobbled in one way or another, most likely due to the abuse they'd endured at the hands of their slave masters. Several others were elderly, sickly or both. While they did have a fair amount of younger people, those of them in that age range had been raised as slaves and clearly never taught to wield a weapon of any sort. The remaining few were older women who were far removed from the shield maidens who sallied forth into battle alongside male warriors in my homeland. No, there would be no assistance in direct battle from these former slaves – at least not anytime soon. While that realization was a blow to my fervent desire to see Osherah burned to the ground, there was a sense of honor in it as well; if I could assist them in freeing other slaves, create some sort of revolt, perhaps I might free Lacina in the ensuing chaos and serve their goal and my own in one decisive victory.

"The Festival of the Serpent is but two nights away, Skarl," Jorgen's powerful voice cut through the chatter of all those present, bringing all eyes on me. "That gives us only today and tomorrow to formulate a plan to rescue your Lacina and spirit you both to the shore, the way we take former slaves to their freedom.

"But, as you've seen, moving from the prison house, across the town and back to the *Down Below* is not a quick, easy journey," he let his words sink in before continuing. "What say you?"

"Tell me more about this festival," my request seemed to stave off his curiosity as to my thoughts.

"It begins with many slave girls dancing for the Ysling Chieftain, Viggo and their Runemaster, Lukas as well as a handful of their most respected warriors. There will be a table set up near the dais, where the Yslings lords will sit and eat as the slave girls amuse them.

"Once the feast is over, the Chieftain will dismiss the slave girls, have the table removed, and then have two of the guards bring Lacina to the altar and bind h-her to the s-sacred columns of O-osherah," he paused for a moment, as it became clear the memories of this happening to his own bride were nearly overwhelming him.

"What then?" I asked, hoping to bring his mind back to the festival timeline.

"Then they will pound the tribal drums that summon the world serpent... the monster will slither its way from the dark woods, onto the altar, where it will rise up and hypnotize Lacina with its serpent's stare. Once she has fallen into a docile state, it will... strike..."

The memory almost seemed more than he could bear, so I wasted no time redirecting his thoughts lest the pain of his past overcome the present.

"And, how many souls are still enslaved in this accursed town?" my question seemed to catch Jorgen and some of the others off guard, judging from the way a few recoiled at the apparent insensitivity of my query and others turned their eyes to Jorgen.

"I'd wager a few hundred, if not more..." Jorgen replied.

"And, how many Ysling warriors?"

"I'd guess twice as many," Jorgen's left hand rubbed the top of his head as his face showed the concentration which told me he was deducing where I was going with this.

"But, these aren't warriors, Skarl," he added before I could reply. "We cannot expect them to do anything other than die under the blades of the Yslings if we ask them to throw off their bonds."

"You are right, Jorgen," I responded as I looked upon a nearby torch which reflected its orange glow in my eyes. "However, if we give the bastards something else to focus on, we may yet free all the slaves before the Yslings realize what's happening."

Jorgen's face split with a smile as he raised one eyebrow and said, "Tell me more..."

+++

A curtain of rusted chains swayed back and forth in front of me, as if blown to and fro by some unseen and unfelt wind that swirled about the dungeon. My breath came in visible wisps of frost that faded before my eyes ere I could draw another. All about me, from side to side, was a creeping darkness that clutched at my very being, seeking to pull me in. But, my focus remained on the figure beyond the curtain.

There she was with rough, corroded iron fetters holding her outstretched arms to the dank stone wall that was rank with oozing slime and slick with moisture dripping down from above. Her ivory skin, golden hair and sapphire eyes contrasted against the surrounding gloom as if the noontime sun was shining in the darkest of midnight skies.

I strained ahead to free Lacina from her imprisonment, but any forward momentum I might gain was countered by an unending number of smoky, formless, obsidian hands that sought to drag me backward into the darkness. It was then I became aware of the ebony sand in my right hand where my axe should have been. Try as I might, I could no more hold the obsidian grains in my grasp than I could keep the darkness at bay.

Our gaze met, and in her eyes I could see the light of hope slowly fading. At this, a rage welled within me as if I might break free from the fingers clutching at my very soul through pure force of will. But, my redoubled efforts were in vain. The harder I sought to surge forward, the further away she seemed to fade, until at once, she was gone and stygian darkness swallowed me whole.

+++

I bolted upright in my bed, eyes wide with feral ferocity, seeking to spy what manner of demons sought to drag me into Hel with them. Looking this way and that, the reality that I'd awoken from yet another nightmare, and I was actually in the cave of the *Down Below*, set in.

As Runemaster, Father would often tell me of prophetic dreams he experienced in times of crisis, or worse, times of peace that were soon ended. Often, he would need to seek out the Seer to interpret these nocturnal visions. But, the meaning of this nightmare was all too clear: time was running out...

+++

A few hours later, and all were awake and moving about in the cave room. Darla and a few other women and children were preparing the morning meal while I sat upon my bed, sharpening my axe. After giving a few orders to some of the other freed slaves, Jorgen came over and sat down next to me.

"I've never seen a blade such as that one, Skarl. Do all the Kirwall Warriors fight with such splendid weapons?"

"No, my friend, there is only one such axe in all the world," I replied, my fondness for the icon coloring my voice. "It is one of nine sacred weapons, forged by the gods themselves and given to the nine Runemasters to mete out justice."

"And, how may I ask," Jorgen plied. "Did you come to possess such a magnificent piece of warcraft?"

"'Twas my Father's and his Father's before him," my answer came on a voice quieted by reminiscence of my lineage. "In fact, every Kirwall Runemaster down through time has wielded this axe." I set down the sharpening stone and ran my fingers across the runes carved into the edge of the blade. "These markings have drank the blood of countless enemies, but more importantly, they've warded off threats more numerous than the stars. For none in the Nir Mountains who has drawn breath is unaware of this axe and the formidability of he who wields it. That knowledge alone often keeps the wolves at bay... the human ones at least.

"Legends tell of its history down through the ages, originally hammered into shape on the forge of Mephis, blacksmith of the gods. Wielded by mythic heroes, famed Runemasters of days past, it was forever destined to enforce the laws of our land and see that justice is done."

"Well then, sounds like you've just the tool for this evening's job," Jorgen laughed as he patted me on the shoulder and walked away to assist another freed slave.

CHAPTER EIGHTEEN: *FESTIVAL OF YSFANG*

Filled with dark clouds, it was only possible to tell the sun was setting in the evening sky due to the rapidly decreasing light in the town square of Osherah. Through the crowd and multitude of dancing slave girls, we could see the Ysling Chieftain, Viggo as he sat at the center of the banquet table, with Lukas the Ysling Runemaster on his right and Tristan Angivar, the traitor, on his left. It was clear from his body language, the way he angled his shoulders, nodded his head and moved his eyes, that he had great trust in Lukas, but was still leery of Tristan. Alas, the three still sat in their apparent joy as if they were attending a grand party. Watching them eat, drink and revel in merriment of the festival made my jaw clench in a manner that might soon grind my teeth to dust.

"Relax, my friend," Jorgen urged, in a tone that sought to soothe my growing rage. "All is prepared, we need only remain patient for a little while longer."

Turning to lock eyes with Jorgen for the briefest of instants, I nodded in acknowledgement of his words before looking around to take inventory of the number of Ysling warriors in the crowd. Large containers of mead were everywhere and while no slaves were allowed to enjoy the strong drink, I was pleased to see none of the Yslings had such restrictions. The more alcohol in their systems when we made our move, the slower their reflexes and the less formidable they were – and the easier it would be for our plan to sow discord among them all. Jorgen and Darla had assured me this festival was as old as the town, and never once had it ever been interrupted, so they had no reason to expect the coming storm.

After a time, Viggo stood and raised his cup, first to Lukas, then to Tristan, before turning to the crowd. While I could see his lips moving, the rising chatter of the revelers made it impossible to make out what he was saying. However, the meaning was quite clear: he was toasting his old and new partnerships and preparing for the main event.

As Viggo finished, everyone at the banquet table stood. The slave girls moved back furtively into the crowd, each one hoping against hope they'd not caught the eye of any of the men at the table. If they had, past festivals gave plenty of evidence that a night of rape and other abuses would surely await them. The thought of one of them forcing themselves on those poor dancers boiled the blood within my veins.

Male slaves came and moved the table away, once the girls were gone from sight, leaving a clearing in front of the dais soon filled by seven men with seven drums. The crowd remained parted where the slaves had taken the table, and soon, four Ysling guards came marching forth from the direction of the prison house, with Lacina in the middle of their formation. They'd clothed her in an ivory, silken, form-fitting gown, not unlike the one from my dream-visions – a fact I'd not realize until much later.

With all eyes on her, I hastily removed my stained cloak, revealing the Ysling armor we'd taken from the guard. Thankfully, the hauberk was bulky enough to hide my axe between it and my chest. Moving stealthily, yet boldly through the crowd so as not to attract attention from other Yslings but also not to appear as if I wasn't one of them, I worked my way to the side of the dais. Thankfully, all eyes were riveted to my love – and why shouldn't they be? Even in this horrid situation, she was the most beautiful woman in sight. The crowd surged forward, each person straining to get a glimpse of the next sacrifice: my heart, Lacina.

They brought her onto the altar and as they tied her left arm to the column, she turned her face towards me for a brief moment. In her eyes I could clearly see the defiance that was only natural in the heart of a Kirwall shield maiden. Her gaze flitted about, from guard to sword to crowd to the roads that led away from the square. It was obvious she was calculating what escape would require of her. After a moment, her supple shoulders lifted and fell in an almost imperceptible sigh, which told me she was accepting the fact that single-handedly gaining her freedom was not possible. Then her eyes raised once again to the scabbard on the nearest guard's belt. My breath caught, fearing her indominable will would suddenly hasten her doom.

In one fluid motion, she jumped toward the left column and with her right hand, pulled the sword from the nearest guard's scabbard. Before he knew she was upon him, his own sword slashed open his throat, spraying blood full upon the left column and the crowd closest to it. However, ere she could pull the blade back for another stroke, the other guards grabbed her and took the weapon from her hands. They contained her fury, tying her to the right column as Viggo and Lukas laughed heartily.

"She is indeed as spirited as you said, friend Tristan!" Viggo exclaimed. He raised his voice even louder so that all in the square would hear his next words. "Pay heed my people to the daughter of Kirwall! She is all that's left of our ancestral enemies! And, before this night ends, her light will go out just like the rest of her filthy clansmen!" As he continued, Lacina fought back, redoubling her efforts at his insults, but she was no match for the four warriors who were binding her to the dais. "What a fierce will she possesses! That fury shall make for a sacrifice truly worthy of Ysfang!"

All in attendance, with the exception of myself, now standing but a few paces from Lacina, and Jorgen, who had moved to the back of the square as planned, erupted in cheering at the Chieftain's words.

With a wave of his right arm, Viggo turned to the seven drummers and gave the next command. "Let the ceremony begin!"

Instantly the drummers began pounding out a rhythmic, tribal beat on their drums, which silenced the crowd. After what seemed an eternity of nothing but the drums disturbing the air, the twisted, black trees behind the altar began to move and quake. It was more the trees trembled with fear than jostled due to the massive creature pushing its way through them. At this new motion, many voices in the crowd gasped and a great number of voices whispering "Ysfang" filled the air.

With her back to the crowd, Lacina was the first to view the world serpent, as its head emerged. It was blacker than the surrounding trees yet glistening in the torchlight and as broad as I was tall. In one sudden movement, it erupted through the trees and onto the altar. Not one to ever show fear in the face of impending doom, Lacina, like all shield maidens would, let out a battle cry that nearly drowned out the drums with its ferocity.

"YYYYIIIIIIAAAAHHHHHHH!"

Apparently, no other sacrifice had ever dared yell at the giant snake, as the sound of her voice seemed to startle it. The beast raised its head upward on its scintillating obsidian body until it was nearly twice my height in the air. The coiled devil's forked tongue shot out over and over, as if it was trying to ascertain if it should strike now or continue seeking to mesmerize its prey with the death stare contained in its blood red eyes.

"HSSSSSSSSSSSSSSS" the sound, like steam escaping a geyser on an ice-covered volcanic slope, permeated the air, silencing everyone in earshot, including the drummers. It seemed even the night sounds quieted in that moment. If it weren't for the serpent's hissing, I might have thought myself suddenly struck deaf.

Then Ysfang began its hypnotic dance, moving rhythmically from side to side as the pounding of the tribal drums started up again, mirroring the serpent's motions. Slowly, the beast pulled the rest of its body onto the altar, one coil after the next. Once fully revealed, it was obvious this thing was lengthier than the largest long boat in our fleet, perhaps, if pulled upward to full height, it might even reach the top of the mast of the *Draugr*, my now deceased friend Edrho's fine ship. I had to admit never before had I seen a beast this large, or more accurately, this long.

Turning my gaze back to Lacina, it became apparent now was the time for action. Her defiance had faded from her lovely face and she seemed to be asleep yet with eyes wide open. The serpent's hypnotic effect was taking hold. Thankfully, Jorgen had discerned the same thing and raised a horn to his lips, blowing a blast from it that shattered the sound of the sacrificial ceremony.

As everyone turned toward the origin of the horn blast, he did as I'd asked and yelled "ATTACK!"

Looking back beyond the edges of the square in all directions, the horizon over the town was covered in an orange tinged smoke that filled the air. Within seconds the source of the smoke was revealed, and the crowd broke into panic at the sight: fires raged all over the town! I took a moment to thank the gods for blessing the feet of the slaves. They were more than willing to do as Jorgen had asked, setting their master's long houses ablaze in a unified uprising.

Chaos erupted!

Everywhere I turned, people ran for the streets leading back into town and most of the Ysling warriors ran with them. The guards who had brought Lacina to be sacrificed, closed ranks around Viggo, Lukas and Tristan. Upon the altar, the serpent lowered its head back to ground level, turning back and forth from Lacina, to the townspeople and the fires raging in the distance.

Sliding my axe from inside my Hauberk, I raised the blade to my lips and whispered the incantation in Old Runish, words that were ancient when the blade was hammered into form. The runes upon its edges glowed with the chant of the berserker spell and then it was my turn to let out a battle cry.

"YYYYIIIIIIAAAAHHHHHHH!"

Leaping onto the altar, I landed squarely between the snake and my love, with my back to her. My sudden appearance seemed to be more than the serpent could take in the chaotic eruption of sensory stimulation from the fires, cries and commotion. Some deep-rooted instinct within the monster took over and it struck out at me with a speed that would shame the fastest snow lion.

Thankfully, I'd anticipated this and had already begun bringing my axe downward between us in a two-handed killing stroke. While my timing was off, the blade still bit into the very tip of the snake's nose, splattering black blood onto the altar and sending the beast recoiling in pain. Vast musculature rippled beneath its obsidian scales as it let forth an unholy cry I'd never heard before and hope to never hear again. The snake scream was the sound of terror incarnate. It sliced into my ears like nails on rock, jolting my nerves. The sound haunts me to this very day.

Wasting no time, I spun around and swung my axe near Lacina, severing the triple-braided cord that held her left arm to the column. As I continued my pivot, I caught an unexpected look upon her face; it was clear she did not recognize me, clothed as I was in the Ysling armor. The helmet upon my head contained my blond braids and partially concealed my face from her. Before I could consider this further, I'd spun around once more and brought my axe up again in a side to side swing meant to split the serpent's head in two.

But my blow met only empty air.

The monster had reared back now, as if trying to discern how best to devour a morsel that bit back. Gauging the distance between myself and the now coiled nightmare, I turned once again and swung full upon the other cord holding Lacina's right arm. Adding further to her surprise, I bellowed a command at her before turning once more to the snake. "Lacina! Behind me!"

"Skarl?!" her voice cut through the din, clearly imparting she recognized mine, even if she was unable to discern my identity from the uniform I wore. She would later tell me she assumed some Ysling cur had stolen my Father's axe and meant to use it to drive Ysfang back into its den since the ceremony had been interrupted.

With my love at my back I faced the beast by moving my axe side to side to match the rhythmic motions of its head. The berserker spell thrummed within my veins as the voices of my ancestors raised above the blood rushing in my ears.

"FINISH IT!" they cried over and over again with every rapid beat of my heart.

It was then the impetuousness of my youth forced me into a mistake. Yelling another battle cry, I launched myself at Ysfang's head, swinging my axe in what would certainly be a death blow could I but connect with the monster's face. However, the speed and fluidity of its movements belied its size. The serpent recoiled away from my swing, awaiting my landing before shooting its tail forward to wrap me its muscular coils.

Lifting me bodily from the ground, the snake sought to squeeze the life out of me with a wave of pulsing constrictions. It had wrapped just below my arms, which remained free. However, due to the placement of its coils, I was unable to move my axe enough to muster a full swing. After a few seconds, I felt and heard the dual crack of what I believed to be two ribs as pain shot through my torso. Once satisfied I could bite it no more with my blade, the beast raised me over its mouth and prepared to devour me. If it weren't for the spell of the berserker, I've no doubt I would have passed out in that very moment, succumbing to the incredible pain and pressure from the snake's constricting coils.

I recall watching the serpent's maw open, exposing countless dagger like teeth that would surely rip the flesh from my bones, including the four fangs, two in the top jaw and two at the bottom – each fang glistened with a greenish saliva I was mildly aware must be some sort of poison or toxin. As it lowered me into reach of those massive jaws. I took the only course of action left to me. Pulling my legs upward into my body, I waited an instant before kicking downward with all my might. Both feet connected with the serpent's lower fangs, knocking one out of its mouth and bending the other inward at an unnatural angle.

The beast once again issued its unholy scream as it writhed in sudden agony. The pain-induced spasms allowed me to regain my freedom and as I dropped from its coils, I brought my axe down into its lower jaw splitting it in twain to match the forked tongue that jetted in and out in anguish.

Landing on my feet I hacked and hewed at the beast with all the pent up fury of the berserker spell, until the serpent's dead body convulsed in involuntary spasms upon the altar. Once I was assured it was no longer a threat, I wiped the black blood from my face and turned to grab Lacina to make good our escape just as planned.

I spun around to find… I was all alone.

There was no one where she had just stood, only a torn piece of her gown!

Frantically casting my eyes through the chaos, I spied her on the other side of the square, trying her best to fight off the grasp of Tristan with both hands tied behind her back. The traitor was dragging her bodily into an alley between two long houses. Rage once again flowed through me as I sought to pursue them.

But, before I could exit the altar, a figure appeared between us, sword drawn with runes etched on the edges of its blade. Lukas, the Ysling Runemaster blocked my path and meant to have revenge of his own for the death of his 'god'. I was at once made aware of the similarities of his blade and my axe, recalling stories Father had told me as a boy that the axe was one of nine weapons, forged for the nine Runemasters to administer justice among the people. Clearly, Lukas had his own brand of justice...

He was an imposing man, grim faced, black maned with a jagged gash running from the back of his neck down the left side of his jaw – clearly a reminder of a battle fought long ago. The lack of pigmentation in the scar made it stand out in great contrast from his grey skin. While his shoulders were not as wide as that of my Father's, he struck as nearly an imposing figure, standing just as tall, exuding a power that could not be ignored. His chain mail was made of some obsidian metal I'd never seen before and about his shoulders hung the black fur of what I could only assume was one of the Helwolves, like those who tried to devour me on the banks of the river a few nights ago.

When he spoke, his voice was like a sledgehammer being dragged across an anvil.

"You shall pay for that, puny boy," he yelled above the din. "It took me ten long years to raise that serpent to replace it's father. And that's how long I intend to see you suffer, cur!"

We circled one another, each looking for an opening to attack. Unable to find a clearly visible physical breach, Lukas instead tried to strike at my inner self. "Tristan told me about you. Impetuous, favored from birth and always protected from real harm by your now dead father," he sneered. "Coddled by the real warriors, every victory handed to you since you're far too pathetic to earn one yourself! The idea that a whelp such as you could carry one of the nine weapons disgusts me! Let me show you what it means to be a *real* Runemaster."

As is characteristic of one casting a spell, Lukas lifted the blade of his long sword to his lips and quickly recited an incantation in Old Runish. When the final word left his mouth, the runes along the blade erupted in a fiery orange glow that quickly faded to crimson. While I didn't fully hear his words, and wouldn't have been wholly familiar with the spell, the sound and sight tugged at a memory deep in my mind.

CHAPTER NINETEEN: *BATTLE OF THE RUNEMASTERS*

The morning sun had yet to lift above the horizon and just as it always did in those moments right before dawn, it felt as if we were in the darkest part of night. Slowly and silently, we slid through the woods, entering one by one into the village of Yorvik. Similar in size to Kirwall, this village had several dozen long houses, a great house, out buildings, merchant carts and more. Unlike Kirwall, however, it had a smell of fish about it – most likely due to its close proximity to the Bay of Essra that fed out to the Galtek Sea. The Yorviks were first and foremost fishermen, but all too often they went to the west to hunt the great stags, often in Kirwall territory.

The evening before, Father had come to me and told me it was time – time for me to earn my blade and my place among the war parties. Time to become a man. Both Runolf and I had already completed the Tolkengaard, our rite of passage, and our first battle was the final test. If the god's saw fit to allow us to join the other Kirwall warriors, they would see that we survived the battle. Despite also passing the Tolkengaard, Tristan was nowhere to be found during preparations or in the battle itself, something I'd never noticed until ruminating on the experience.

As Runolf and I waited with anticipation, Sigurd Angivar, our chieftain, informed us of the crime. With fire in his eyes and vengeance on his heart, our Chieftain called us to arms.

"Long have we suffered the stench of the Yorviks staining the land with their very existence," Sigurd, a man easily given to anger, bellowed with his deep, rich voice loud enough for all to hear. "Long have we had an uneasy truce with them, meant to allow both peoples to co-exist so neither would grow weak enough to fall under the might of the Yslings, Ahsgulians or other warring clans.

"This very morning, the Yorviks defiled our truce, spilling the life of Mikkel Helvig and his hunting party into the virgin snow," he paused a moment to allow those words to sink in. "And for that, they. will. pay!"

Mikkel was a friend of sorts, though we were never as close as Runolf and I were. He was the son of Kjell Helvig, Father's best friend. And Kjell was our clans' mightiest warrior and the one tasked with training the young men to become warriors. Aside from Sigurd, Father, the Seer and Einar Jor'Heim, there was no one more important in Kirwall than Kjell Helvig and Skadiya Ulthor, the shield maiden trainer.

While we'd had an uneasy peace with our eastern neighbors for generations, it was not unheard of for clashes and confrontations to arise between

...ENTERING ONE BY ONE INTO THE VILLAGE...

Kirwall and Yorvik, primarily over incursions into each other's territories often driven by a need for food in the harsh winters. Normally, the Chieftains would meet and work out some form of reparation, but not this time.

The death of Kjell's son, who was also Einar Jor'Heim's protégé, brought more insult than Sigurd and my Father could bear. There would be no reparation for this other than the spilling of blood on Yorvik soil. Within minutes of learning of Mikkel's death, we were all making preparations in the Kirwall square, war parties were raised and Kjell was drawing up a plan of attack with fire in his eyes and thunder in his voice.

As this was my first raid, I knew not what to expect, but Father tasked me with following Kjell's lead. Runolf was with us, but accompanied his father, in Einar Jor'Heim's group of warriors. While it was wise to keep us in separate parties, Runolf and I had to admit we'd long dreamed of our first trip into battle – together – and being separated brought with it a small amount of childish disappointment. Thankfully, we were both mature enough to keep that to ourselves.

Kjell's group was comprised of seven warriors, five seasoned fighters, Kjell and me. Just as we slipped from the woods into the edge of the village, Kjell halted us. Holding his right hand out and motioning to the ground, he silently commanded us to stand fast. He slid around the corner of the long house we were behind, long knife in hand and a moment later I heard the sound of his blade slicing through flesh before seeing the Yorvik guard's body hit the ground – slowed by Kjell, so the now dead man's armor wouldn't make any noise.

Kjell motioned forward and we moved on, seeking to reach the village square at the same time as the other war parties. We'd dispatched most of the night watchmen we had encountered, but as Kjell was sliding up behind what we believed to be the final one, a horn blared out in the night: someone in the village had detected our presence and sounded the alarm! I would later learn the Runolf had accidentally stepped into view of a guard just before Einar was in position to dispatch the Yorvik warrior. The sounding of the horn was the guard's last act before Einar sent him to the afterlife.

At the blaring horn blast, the village instantly erupted in sounds of battle, screams of women and children and the clash of steel. Kjell urged us forward and we rushed into the square, emerging between two merchant carts and into the chaos of the fight that raged all around.

With a need to see his son avenged, Kjell tore into a group of Yorvik warriors like a man possessed. Would that I could have sat and witnessed the fight, I'm sure I would have learned more about single combat in those next few moments than I ever had in any one lesson from Kjell back home. However, before I could even react, he had downed three opponents and was pressing a fourth.

At what point I do not recall, as the battle was far more intense than a young one of my age ever imagined, I found myself separated from Kjell. While I fought off several Yorvik warriors, each gained the upper hand on me at some point or another, only to have one of our own warriors' step between us and finish them for me. Just as I'd learned to swim by Father tossing me off a cliff into deep waters – which was far more daunting than wading in the shallows, all the combat training in my life couldn't fully prepare me for the frenzy of actual battle.

It wasn't long before I stumbled over something on the ground and looked down for an instant. There in the blood-stained soil lay Kjell's head, his body nowhere to be seen. Time stood still for an instant as I stared into the now lifeless eyes of Father's best friend, a man I'd known – and respected greatly – all my life. I could see his eyes were not focused back upon me, but seemed to stare through the veil, into the Grand Hall of the Gods, where his soul was sure to be taken when the Val'kyree arrived. I would later learn his own rage was his undoing as Kjell failed to follow his own rule: never let your emotions dictate your actions in battle. But, he had taken such account of the Yorviks they would later tell tales of the beast-man who fought with the Kirwall raiders that day.

This moment of shock, surprise and retrospection at the life of Kjell was almost my undoing! I was roused from my thoughts by the deafening crash of blade on blade directly next to my right ear. Recoiling and turning toward the sound, I saw it: Father's axe blocking a Yorvik blade from splitting my skull in twain. Father kicked out at the enemy who sought to lay me low, planting his massive foot in the other man's chest, sending him tumbling backwards into a pile of the dead.

Before I could react, Father grabbed me on the back with his left hand and propelled me at the warrior will all his might. "Finish him!" he bellowed at me.

Through more twist of fate than intentional strike, the force of my Father's push along with my poorly executed attempt to lift my blade to strike saw the tip of my sword dig into the Yorvik warrior's gut, just below his chest plate. His lifeblood sprayed out, catching me in the face. The warm splatter of crimson fluid upon my eyes and lips seemed to fully awaken the warrior spirt within me, as I pulled the sword back and delivered a death thrust Kjell had me practice a thousand times before.

Turning back to Father, my eyes looked around and took inventory of our situation. Kjell and the other men from our party were all dead around us. The fighters Father had entered with were nowhere to be seen. We were surrounded by seven Yorvik warriors, yet none of them advanced on us, seeming to remain satisfied that we not leave.

A moment later I learned why.

Pushing his way between two of the fighters in front of us, a barrel-chested, mountain of a man emerged onto the scene. He carried a single-bladed axe, one with runes inscribed in the edge of the blade, just like Father's.

"Jarl Kirwall!" he spat my Father's name out as if it were poison. "Ever have I dreamed of this moment. You, here, about to die on my blade. Your axe, mine, once and for all."

Ignoring his insulting tone and words, Father lifted the blade of his axe to his lips and whispered an incantation in Old Runish. At once the runes ignited in blaze of orange that instantly faded to crimson. He then let out a Kirwall battle cry and leapt across the distance between himself and the Yorvik Runemaster.

Their axes clashed again and again as Father sought to wear down his opponent. The other man seemed taken aback at the sheer ferocity of Father's attack. After several successful parries and counter strikes, Father's axe slipped past his guard and bit into his left shoulder. A look of sheer agony exploded across the man's face, far more than one might expect from the non-fatal flesh wound Father had managed to inflict.

As the Yorvik Runemaster recoiled in pain, Father pressed the advantage, hammering the man farther and farther back with a ferocious volley of swings. Clearly, the wound on the left shoulder had somehow sapped the other man of strength as he seemed to grow weaker with each violent crash of their axes.

Ducking below a counter swing, Father crouched onto his left heel – as he had taught me to do many winters before, and spun around with all his might, both hands clutching the haft of his axe, bringing it around in circle that ended as he chopped both legs out from under his opponent.

Before the other Runemaster's body hit the ground, Father was among the rest of the Yorvik men, hacking and chopping. I wasted no time joining him and there we stood, Father and son, fighting off the remaining seven warriors. It seemed but an instant before I vanquished the third foe in front of me and realized all that remained in the clearing was my Father and I, and a pile of souls ready for the Val'kyree's harvest.

Hours later, after we'd reunited with the other Kirwall warriors and fully sacked the Yorvik village, we made our way back to Kirwall. Father, clearly exhausted by the aftereffects of his battle spell, and somehow in great pain even though he had but minor scratches and bruises from the fighting, spoke with Einar Jor'heim for a time. The two men assessed the losses of more than a dozen warriors, including Kjell, and counted the spoils gained in the raid. All the while I was overcome with a need to know. What was that spell Father cast? I'd never seen his blade glow that way before, nor ever heard him mention such an incantation. And, why was he in such obvious pain? While he had already taught me the berserker spell, the healing spell, and spoken of several others, this was the first I'd learned of this one.

Finally, he and I rode side by side.

"You have much to learn about battle, Skarl," Father admonished me. "Had I not been there, you'd surely be in the Grand Hall of the Gods right now, alongside Mikkel, Kjell and our other warriors lost this day."

My shoulders dropped and my gaze fell to the ground at his words, like most sons I wanted to please Father with my prowess. Clearly, I'd failed in my inaugural battle.

"However, it was your first fight," he continued. "And, you lived to tell of it." With that he reached out and clapped me on the back, giving me a smile that showed he was proud of me, despite the mistakes I'd made. "Adon and the other gods are smiling upon my son!" I basked in the warm feeling of his praise for but a moment before a compulsion to know came over me.

"Father," I couldn't contain my curiosity any longer. "The words you spoke in Old Runish over your blade. I've never heard them before."

His lips clamped together as his brow furrowed and a darkness seemed to fall over his eyes, washing away the joy they'd just held. Several moments passed before he answered.

"Tis the *spell of blood*, young Skarl."

"'*Spell of blood*?'" I repeated his words to commit them to memory. "Why have you never told me of this before?"

"There are some spells better left uncast, such as this one. A handful of incantations you only call upon if you see no other road to victory," he explained in a somber tone. "The spell of blood is a combination of the berserker spell, which gives the caster heightened strength, speed, dexterity and reflexes as well as a lessened sensation of pain, and something more. The spell of blood also brings a Hel fire that ignites the blood of anyone struck by the blade."

"That is why the Yorvik Runemaster seemed so affected by your initial blow!"

"Yes, my son," Father replied. "It is my understanding that every drop of blood within the body burns like a roaring inferno. That level of pain alone might kill a lesser man. Unfortunately, the agony is also radiated backward to a lesser extent through the wielder of the spell," his jaw tightened, and a quick inhalation shot through his nostrils as our horses stumbled a bit in a depression along the trail, as if to accentuate his point. "And, until the caster is recovered from the effects of the spell, the blood fire remains burning within."

Not one to openly admit to pain or any other sign of weakness, Father stopped there and did not say another word for some time. However, the grimace on his face and occasional wincing when we went through any rough patch in the terrain told me all I needed to know. It would be months before Father seemed fully recovered, if he ever really was…

+++

The metal sheathed haft of my axe drew sparks from Lukas' blade as I parried a blow meant to sever my head from the rest of me. Quickly pushing down on his blade, I jabbed outward with my left fist, landing only a glancing blow on his chin. This elicited a wry smile from my adversary as he withdrew his sword and brought it back up in an effort to take advantage of my apparent overreach in punching him.

Fortunately for me, he had to draw the blade full across his body to pull back for another swing. Knowing I could not parry another blow so quickly, I kicked outward with my right foot and let out a battle cry, the blow sent him backward just far enough to regain my composure.

"Kicking and screaming?" Lukas laughed in a mocking tone. "Exactly what I'd expect from a child…"

He was clearly trying to push me to a rage that would see my decision making left aside for unthinking, anger driven actions. However, the rush of the fading berserker spell still filled my ears which made his words enter my mind like a far-off cry in a half-remembered dream. Ever mindful of the effects of allowing the rune sword to penetrate my guard, I concentrated more on it, than the long knife. If he had indeed cast the *spell of blood* and I allowed that blade to cut me, I'm not sure I would overcome the grizzled old Runemaster.

We parried and countered, swung, evaded and chopped at one another for what seemed an eternity. But, try as I might I could not get past his defenses. Thankfully, he'd not worked through mine either, but the longer this fight ensued the further Tristan would take Lacina from me. My thoughts turned to her for an instant, which was nearly a fatal mistake. Involuntarily glancing in the direction where I'd last seen her, my eyes came off Lukas for a fraction of an instant which was all he needed.

That he was aware of how focused I'd been on his ancient blade was obvious. With his right hand, he slashed the rune sword to my left, which drew my attention back from where Lacina had been. Unfortunately, my eyes failed to see his left hand, which had pulled a long knife from his belt and used it to slash at my face. The tip of his blade bit into my jaw at the left side of my chin and ripped upward diagonally across my lips and through my cheek before exiting my flesh just above my right eye. If I had not involuntarily pulled my head backward at the first instant of impact, the blow might have been fatal. As it was, blood mixed with sweat, poured into my right eye and blinded it. While I didn't immediately feel the pain of the blow, the sweat and blood now in my eye burned, causing me to recoil in a rotational manner, which I'm sure is all that saved me from the decapitating blow Lukas swung with his rune sword as a follow up.

Like a young, wounded snow lion fighting a pack of wolves, I parried and shrunk back as he sent a volley of blows down on me, clearly hoping to finish this once and for all. It was then I determined to use his tactics against him.

"You flail about like a boy who knows not how to fight back against a bully, Lukas," I sneered. "Surely, if you were as mighty as you claim, I would be dead by now. No, I think you are old… pathetic… weak."

A look of rage burned in his eyes at my taunt, and I pushed further. Knowing the spell of blood did not provide the full heightened physical traits the berserker spell provided, I sought to draw him in further, letting him believe more pain gripped me than truly did. I allowed my shoulders to sag and back stepped with my right foot, dragging my left backward while keeping it between us. This sort of kick-slide, as Father had called it, was a defensive retreat that provided a smaller target for the opponent than squared off shoulders, while allowing the defender to deliver a mighty blow with the right arm.

Lukas stepped in, swinging successive blows with the rune sword and long knife. I allowed his smaller weapon to cut into my thigh and faked an expression of great pain when it did. A smile played across his face and he lifted his rune sword on high, preparing for a blow that would have broken a weakened warrior's defenses and split my skull.

Just as his sword was at the apogee of its arc, I lunged forward suddenly grabbing his sword arm right below the elbow, which left his torso unguarded. With all the strength still in me, I rotated my hips and brought my axe around in a shortened swing that ended deep in Lukas' side, the blade parting flesh, ribs and more than one internal organ.

The impetus of my blow was too much for Lukas' suddenly weakened frame and we bowled over with him landing full on his back. Before he could bring his left arm up to reach me with the long knife, I stomped down on his left wrist. The snapping of bones accompanied my step and ere he could utter another sound, I swung full into his chest, burying my axe in his vile heart.

Once I was assured Lukas drew breath no more, I grabbed his rune sword, and spun around to pursue Tristan and Lacina.

The slaves had done their part masterfully, as most of the town was in flames now, with smoke choking the air in a death grip. All about were people running around chaotically. With no real idea of where they might have gone, I moved to the prison house where Lacina had been kept. Just as I was about to enter the street in front of it, a hand grabbed me from behind, yanking me into the shadows.

CHAPTER TWENTY: *THE OLD FORT*

"Skarl! It's me!" Jorgen blurted, holding his hands up to ward off the killing blow I'd raised in response to his attempt to manhandle me.

Wasting no time with pleasantries, I immediately sought answers. "Where is she? Where is Lacina?"

"She was here just a few moments ago," Jorgen asserted. "I was going to follow them when I spied you coming."

"Which way did she go?"

"Tristan and several Ysling warriors had her and they were headed for the docks."

"Which way, man!" I demanded with far too much impatience.

"Follow me," Jorgen motioned and ran off down the street.

Within a few moments we crested the hillside and noted the road led down to the waters some distance below. Among the throngs of merchants and slaves moving towards the water to escape the fires, we noted Tristan, Lacina and five Ysling warriors – they were almost to the docks.

Running as fast as we could, we had to deal with the throngs of people who impeded our every step. This delay allowed our quarry to board a long boat before we were halfway down the hill.

"Where are they going?" my question hammered the air.

"Across the river, see the clearing? There's an old fort over there, built ages ago to withstand sieges from invaders. I've never known it to be used in my time here, but the stories say it was nigh impenetrable. These days, it mostly lies in ruins. However, they could still hold us at bay from inside."

"Then we must prevent them from gaining egress!" I demanded, redoubling my efforts to make it to the docks. There were several other boats pulling away from the shore as we reached them, most heading down river. Some were full of now freed slaves, some with merchants and a one with Ysling warriors. Only the Yslings moved in the same direction as Tristan.

The enemy warriors hadn't moved their boat more than a sword length from the dock as Jorgen and I leapt onboard. My axe ended two of them before they ever even realized we were among them. The other three turned in surprise and one went down immediately with Jorgen's sword tip lodged in his gut. Silently, the other two and I fought, as they retreated to the bow of the boat. I feinted toward the one on my right, just as he stepped into a coil of rope. My sudden lunge at him sent him backward, where he lost his footing and then tumbled overboard.

Pulling my axe back from the swipe at the one who fell in the water, I blocked the blow from the remaining Ysling with Lukas' rune sword, leaving him open to the death blow from my axe. With every precious second I was fully aware of the growing distance between us and Lacina.

"Quick man! Row for your life!" I bellowed at Jorgen as I jumped down and grabbed an oar in each hand and pulled for all I was worth.

Quick glances backward showed that Tristan's craft would make landfall about a minute ahead of us, giving them enough time to race to the old fort well before we could stop them. To his credit, Jorgen pulled the oars with all the might I'd ever seen from my fellow clansmen when we'd gone out on the water in my youth. Behind us, Osherah burned on the hilltop, a sight that gave me a modicum of satisfaction in that moment. Now Viggo and his remaining clansmen knew the price of testing Kirwall. For the briefest of instants, I imagined Father looking down on the flames and laughing at our enemies. Then my mind turned back to the task at hand.

As if he knew my thoughts, Jorgen spoke up. "We should expect Viggo and his guard to already shelter in the fort," he stated with grim certitude. "The odds are not in our favor one bit, my friend."

Turning to him with a wry smile, I replied in the only way a Kirwall warrior could. "Then they better have brought a full supply of pyre wood."

Turning to me to reply, Jorgen's eyes went wide and his hand shot out to point in the direction we headed. "LOOK!"

Turning to follow his amazed stare, I saw her in all her glory. There on the deck of the other boat was Lacina, bloody sword in hand, with two dead Ysling warriors at her feet. The spirit of Kirwall burned within her still!

"ROW MAN!" I bellowed at Jorgen, seeing our chance to catch them ere they made landfall.

The other boat floundered as the Yslings gave up their oars in an effort to subdue the ferocious shield maiden, who was now among them like a wild cat in a hen house. We were closing the gap between us rapidly and once we were within a few boat lengths, I heard Tristan's voice above the clang of clashing swords.

"Do not kill her! Viggo wants her alive!" Tristan roared at them.

Seeing my chance, I dropped the oars and slashed a rope free from the rigging of our boat. The other end went to the top of the mast. Wasting no time, I ran toward the back of the boat with all I still had within me. At the last second, before I hit the stern, I leapt outward to the left, with both hands gripping the rope as if my life depended on it – since Lacina's did!

I swung outward on the rope, to the port side, before the line pulled taut and angled me toward the front of our boat in a wide arc. Thankfully, I'd timed it just right and rope reached the end of its sweep away from our craft close enough to the Yslings that I was able to let go and fly through the air the last distance to land firmly on the stern of their boat.

While my muscles ached and felt the weight of the after-effects of the berserker spell I'd cast in the town square, I summoned every ounce of strength remaining and waded into the Yslings from behind.

Lacina's countenance lit up like the summer solstice when she saw me upon the deck, hewing through the warriors that separated us. Within a moment, only she, Tristan and I remained. However, the traitor had managed to work his way to her side in the battle and as she felled the last Ysling with a powerful thrust that left her sword lodged in the warrior's chest, Tristan was upon her, seizing her from behind and digging the blade of his dagger into her throat.

"Skarl Kirwall!" He spat my name out as if it left an unbearable taste in his mouth. "I should have known you would follow us here. Take one more step and I'll spill her blood all over the deck of this ship and your journey will be for naught!"

Locking eyes with Tristan, I knew he was many things: a warrior, a coward, a traitor, but in this instant, I had no doubt he would add murderer to his list of qualities were I not to comply.

"Now, sit at the oars and pull! We're heading ashore and you're going to get us there or Lacina dies a mere few feet from your grasp!"

"Don't listen to him Skarl!" Lacina blurted. "This cur doesn't have the intestinal fortitude to kill a shield maiden! The gods do not welcome murderers into the Grand Hall!"

"Do not test me woman!" Tristan replied. The flesh on her neck turned a stark white where he pulled the knife inward further, before the trickle of blood ran down her throat onto her white gown.

Knowing, despite her efforts to compel me to action, I had little choice but to comply with Tristan's demand. I sat on the bench closest to me, grabbed an oar in each hand and began to row towards the shore. Behind me I noted Jorgen, still in the other craft, was not as close as I'd expected. In fact, he and the other boat I'd just launched from were moving down river, away from us. Had he abandoned me now, in my moment of need? Perhaps he saw the hopelessness of our predicament and was using this chance to finally gain his own freedom? And, for that I could not blame him.

"Faster dog!" Tristan order before I heard, then felt him spitting upon me.

It wasn't long before I could hear other voices behind us. Turning to glance in the direction we were moving, I saw Viggo and a dozen of his warriors standing on the shore, awaiting us.

"Well done, Tristan Angivar!" the Ysling Chieftain bellowed. "Now we shall have revenge on the one who dared to defile Ysfang and the sacred sacrifice – it's our only hope of appeasing the gods after we allowed this cur to stop the ceremony."

As the bow of our craft slid up onto the shore, four Ysling warriors jumped aboard. Three pinned my arms while the fourth took my weapons. They tied my hands behind my back and handed the rune sword and axe to Tristan. He admired Father's blade for a moment before muttering, almost to himself.

"I've always wondered what it felt like to wield such a weapon…"

"You were never worthy, Tristan the *Traitor*!" I spat at him. "If only you had been born of Einar Jor'Heim or Kjell Helvig, instead of your own father —perhaps then you might have had the stock of a true warrior instead of a politician."

A look of eternal hatred blazed in his eyes at my words and before I knew it, the axe blade was at my throat. "Pick your next words carefully, 'Runemaster,' for they very well may be your last!"

"Tristan!" Viggo's voice cut through the tension like my axe through flesh – thankfully not that of my throat! "Come, we need him alive for the sacrifice!"

The Yslings had also tied Lacina's hands behind her back and were driving us both before them down a path into the thick, black woods. The twisted, gnarled branches of obsidian trees, just like the ones on the opposite bank, quickly blocked what little light the night sky afforded us as we were forced down the trail towards the old fort.

"If this night is the one the gods chose to invite me into the Grand Hall," Lacina pushed against me gently with her shoulder as we marched on. "I take great satisfaction in knowing you are by my side, Skarl."

"I, as well, Lacina," hearing her voice and speaking with her for the first time in many moons gave me a resurgence of strength and energy. I'd scarcely noted my will to live had slowly been fading, but simply being near her was like breathing fresh air after too many hours down in the dank, Nir Caverns. While the exhaustive effects of the berserker spell would not completely run their course until the following evening, her presence provided a renewed lust for living. "But, I've no interest in giving my life to the putrid Ysling gods this night, nor yours."

"Hahaha!" Tristan's laugh shattered the moment Lacina and I shared, offering another reminder of his vile presence. "How pathetic that you still refuse to accept your fate, Skarl. You may have always gained victory throughout our youth, but those days, those childhood games were just that – the arena of children," he paused for a moment before continuing. "While you may have become a man last winter, your adult life ends tonight."

My eyes moved to Lacina as we exchanged a glance that spoke volumes. She had suffered his unwanted attentions since we were old enough to know what such things were. More than once in our teenage years he'd tried to force himself on her, doing so unbeknownst to prying eyes so that she could not rightfully accuse him of such things. The word of a full-fledged shield maiden carried great weight in our clan, but the assertions of a girl against the Chieftain's son would not only fall on deaf ears, it would cast great disrepute on her entire family. So, she suffered his unwanted attentions in silence, with only Runolf and myself aware of what was truly happening. I sought my father's help in this at one point, but he simply replied that if it was the truth the gods would see justice done; Tristan would pay for his heinous acts.

We soon entered a clearing that opened up to the front of the old fort. Massive double doors, several heads taller than I, hewn from logs thicker than my body, greeted us. The surrounding walls were stacked stone. While the forest seemed to try its best to reclaim the wood and stone structure, causing quite a bit of disrepair noted in the vine covered doors and various crumbled stones, it was easy to see that this once had been a magnificent structure. Jorgen was right, before neglect took hold, this must have truly been an impenetrable house.

Two of the Ysling warriors cut some vines away from the front steps and forced the doors open, which took considerable effort on their part. The massive portals swung outward, bottoms scraping through the under-brush that had grown up at the entrance as the rusty hinges groaned in protest.

"Light the torches!" Viggo commanded. One by one the warriors lit the torches inside and the flames upon them flickered and danced, casting eerie shadows down the stone hallways.

The Ysling chieftain motioned down a side hallway which quickly descended into darkness down a set of moss-covered stairs, then barked another order. "Take them to the pits!"

One warrior grabbed a torch from the wall and led us down into the depths, as four more followed behind to ensure we complied. We moved this way and that, changing direction so many times I was sure I'd never find my way back out. After what seemed like a nigh endless number of turns and crossing junctions, we came upon a cell door. Taking a key from a post on the wall opposite the cell door, the lead Ysling unlocked the portal and it swung open as the ancient, corroded hinges groaned in pro-test. The others forced us inside before he slammed it shut once more.

I was able to take quick stock of the cell, and what little there was within. The floor was covered in dried weeds and hay; the walls were the same stone as the rest of the fort, and a lone bench wide enough for a small person to lay upon, sat against the back wall. Using the key to lock us in, a sinister laugh escaped the Ysling's lips as he returned the key to the post on the wall. As one, the warriors turned and moved back into the maze of hallways. Within moments the retreating glow of their torch faded from sight, slowly plunging us into total darkness.

+++

My mental fingers traced the door where the lock was, trying to devise any means by which I might open it without the key. Once I accepted the fact this was a fruitless endeavor, my mind raced from idea to idea, trying desperately to concoct a way we could reach the key on the opposite wall and regain our freedom. Could I use my belt? No, the distance was too vast. Perhaps the rope they'd used to bind our hands? If I could dislodge the key from the post, in total darkness, how would I get it from the floor out of my reach, close enough to grab it?

And, once we were freed from the cell, how were we to make our way out through the pitch-black maze of hallways? The idea of wandering around in these lightless corridors for ages sent a reflexive shiver down my spine. What horrible mind had devised such a place as this? I could see now that the maze and the darkness could easily rob anyone of hope, plunging one into a nightmare of depressed thought they might never return from were they left here for any real amount of time.

As that thought hit me, I flinched involuntarily as something touched my hands, still tied behind my back.

"Don't tell me you're afraid of the dark, '*mighty warrior*,'" Lacina's playfully mocking tone brought a quick smile to my face. "Stand still so I can untie you."

Her fingers moved nimbly, pulling, tugging, working the knot that bound my hands. I've no idea how long it took her as I lost myself for an instant in the intoxicating scent of the woman I loved. Memories of the first time I'd ever had such feelings for her danced through my mind, quickly replaced by the memory of when I learned she shared the same feelings for me. Then, the moment of our first kiss. We guarded our affections in secret as teenagers are want to do, although for the life of me I could not remember what we feared in others knowing.

As she made one last pull, I felt my hands come free. Spinning around, I embraced her, planting a passionate kiss upon her full lips. I must admit, I wanted to lose myself in that moment, stop time, forget our dire situation and simply bask in the feelings we had for one another. The touch of her flesh pressed against mine was more than enough to sustain me forever, or so I thought. Thankfully, while she felt the same way, Lacina broke the embrace.

"There's enough time for that later, my love," she murmured in a playfully delicious tone that set my heart afire. She was a woman of fiery passion, never one to accept defeat, always looking for a way to work the outcome to her advantage. While that might sound selfish, she was anything but, always seeking to improve the lives of those she cared for. "Untie me so we can discern a means of escape."

Turning her around quickly, my grasp slid down her arms to the knots that bound her hands. I worked in total darkness, and must admit, my mind lost focus every time my fingers slipped from the knots and moved across her sensuous flesh. A blazing passion for her consumed me, and I wanted nothing more than to take her in that moment. But her previous words rang true; there would be time for our love after we made good our escape, the gods willing.

A few moments later she was able to pull her hands free. Wheeling about, she reached up, and grabbed my face passionately. Her left thumb gently traced the jagged wound left behind by Lukas' long knife before her fingers pulled my head towards her. We shared another passionate kiss, then embraced for several moments, allowing our spirits to fill one another with renewed vigor. As before, I didn't want this moment to end and was once again losing myself in her arms when she pulled away just enough to pose the question.

"What now, warrior? How are we to make good our escape?"

"Adon has blessed my quest thus far, surely he will continue to do so," I replied. "Now, let's find a way out."

Turning away from her I went back to the door, my fingers exploring every iota of the door's surface, the hinges, the frame around it. After some time, I felt assured there was no way to get through the portal without the key that was just beyond our reach. Knowing it was hanging but a few steps away seemed another cruel machination of whatever monster designed this dungeon. The knowledge of the means to freedom lying just beyond one's grasp drove me to an almost frenzied state. Thankfully, the logical part of my mind took over; convincing me that concern with the key was but another form of torture. And so, I put it from my mind.

My fingers then moved beyond the door and began tracing the walls. Made from rough stone blocks of non-uniform size, each approximately twice the height and width of my hand. A coarse mortar filled the gaps between the blocks. Perhaps here might lie our means of escape? If I could find a place where the mortar was weak, crumbling, I could hasten its failure and remove the block it sealed. If I could get one block out, it would be child's play to remove enough to secure our means of escape.

I know not how long my fingers traced the mortar lines, but I worked my way from floor to ceiling, rotating to my right after tracing all the lines in one spot. After some time, Lacina tired and sought the small bench to sit upon. While she possessed an indominatable spirit, clearly the events of the past few weeks had taken a heavy toll on her spirit.

Before long I heard her breathing slow and adopt a rhythmic pace,

"MY FINGERS...BEGAN TRACING THE WALLS."

indicating she had fallen asleep. That she was exhausted was evident. What hellish tortures had Tristan, Lukas and the other Yslings inflicted on her? If nothing else, I doubt she felt safe enough to sleep much at all since the morning she was taken from Kirwall. Thankfully, my presence seemed to comfort her enough to bring a sense of security that allowed her to rest.

Listening to her regular, peaceful breathing became something of a song in my mind. It reminded me of the chants made during our ceremonies, particularly those performed when we sought the blessing of the gods for spring harvest. I listened to her breathing, the only sound in this forsaken place, and continued tracing the mortar lines. Unfortunately, I'd yet to encounter any that felt as if they would provide an advantage to removing the surrounding block.

For what seemed like hours, I continued my task, top to bottom, left to right, my fingers rubbed across the lines. After a time, I noted the mortar began to feel warm and wet. This puzzled me at first, perhaps there was a hot spring above leaking down the wall? Instinctively pulling my right hand to my face, I inhaled through my nostrils once my fingertips were directly before them. The smell that struck me was all too familiar: blood. It would seem my incessant tracing of the rough mortar had worn through the calloused skin on my fingertips and several of them were now bleeding.

Despite this, I had no choice but to continue tracing the outlines of the blocks. After some time I'd bumped into the small bench that Lacina slept upon. Thankfully, my collision with the lone piece of furniture in the cell did not wake her.

I moved past the bench carefully so as not to wake her, before I continued tracing further. The pain in my bloody fingertips was nothing compared to the wound on my face or cut on my thigh, but it had an annoying quality that grated on my nerves the longer I went. However, I knew giving up would be to embrace the futility of our situation.

After what seemed an eternity, my bloodied fingertips encountered something metallic. My heart leapt at this. How had I not seen whatever this was when we were first ushered into the cell? What was it? Some sort of portal? Could this be the way out I'd been after for what seemed like hours now? Quickly my fingers traced the metal object and after a moment or two the realization grasped my heart, dragging it down into despair: the object was the doorway by which we'd entered the cell. I'd worked my way around the entirety of the room and found nothing of use.

+++

For the first time since Runolf and I had left Kirwall, a feeling of uncon-
querable hopelessness came upon me. As if some unseen force were driving
me down, I sunk to my knees, feeling totally defeated. For once, it would
seem, I could not will my way to victory. While I'd lost many a mock battle
against stouter opponents during the training of my youth, Father had
always exhorted me to never accept defeat.

"You do not lose until you give up, Skarl!" Father was fond of saying.
And, there was great wisdom in those words. But at this moment, they rang
hollow in my heart. Why had the gods allowed me to come this far, only
to rot in this darkened hellhole? Was this the cruel fate they'd planned for
me all along? The very idea of that brought great anger rising up within
me. I felt my jaw clench, my brow furrow as my teeth ground together.
Blood rushed in my ears as it always did when I entered battle, but this
time there was no one to fight, no way to achieve physical victory over my
opponent. Maybe I needed to accept the notion that for once in his miser-
able life, Tristan had won…

A small part of me felt happy for him and that small part curled the left
side of my mouth upward in an ironic smile. Perhaps if Tristan had fared
better in our youth, he might not have felt driven to betray us all? Perhaps
if I'd allowed him to win at some point or another, the desire to hand us
all over to the Yslings never would have burned in his breast? It was at that
moment I wondered if I had created the very traitor who was the undoing of our people. Was all this my fault? Had my unending need to win,
to hear Father's praise, to bask in the adoration of our people come at the
cost of Tristan's heart?

"This is not your fault, Skarl," Her presence at my shoulder startled me
at first. I was unaware she'd awoken, but not surprised she could sense
my mental state. Lacina possessed a keen sense of the heart of others and
was often able to assuage sadness and lift the spirits of those around her.
"Tristan was rotten from birth. Honestly, I should have seen this coming
and, in looking back, I wasn't surprised the morning they burned Kirwall,
it was as if I expected Tristan to have orchestrated it and as soon as I saw
him with the Yslings, I knew – like I'd always known – he was the bane
of our very existence. From the first time he tried to force himself on me,
I knew…"

A deep sigh escaped my lips as we embraced once more.

"If the gods mean to end us here in this dark place, at least we're together,"
she whispered in my ear.

With nothing else to do, I allowed myself to get lost in her embrace, her scent filling my nostrils, her warmth filling my flesh, her presence making me feel whole once more.

After a while, I told her of my vain efforts to discover a weak point in the cell walls. I mentioned the key, just beyond our reach with no means of grasping it. Stopping short of spelling out just how hopeless our situation was, I let my words trail off.

"Then, we shall wait for them to return for us – no matter if it's days, weeks or months," she replied. "And when they do, we shall set upon them with all the fury Clan Kirwall has left in our beating hearts!"

Not only did I love her verve, but, as clearly there was no other means of escape available to us, this plan gave us something to hold onto, aside from each other.

Time seemed to vacillate in this place – were we there for hours? Days? However long we lingered, after some great amount of time, we had both come to the conclusion that perhaps the Yslings had forgotten us. We leaned against the bars of the door, holding hands since we could not gaze upon each other. Neither had spoken for some time and the silence had become all consuming.

And then it was broken.

"KL-clank!"

As one, we turned towards the source of the sound. The slightest hint of light outlined the bench at the back of the cell. At first, I could not tell if it was simply my mind playing tricks on me or not. But, as the glow brightened, the hackles on the back of my neck stood up and the warrior blood ignited in my veins. A dragging noise, as if someone were pulling a body across rocks cast an eerie tone into the air. Moving Lacina behind me defensively, I set my feet and prepared to meet whatever new horror the Yslings sought to unleash upon us in the depths of their prison. Was the maze, hanging key and eternal darkness not enough? Were they so devilish as to beset some blackened horror from the depths on their prisoners? Could it be another serpent, come to exact revenge for the death of Ysfang? My mind raced to the encounter with the ice worm, the death of Runolf, the bestial nightmare that haunted the very caves we played in as children. Perhaps, if not another Ysling snake, we were about to be set upon by one of the ice worm's kin – or worse!

"KL-CLANK!" The noise repeated, but this time far louder, eliciting an almost imperceptible gasp from Lacina. The orange glow suddenly increased greatly, momentarily blinding us as our eyes had grown accustomed to the stygian darkness. Blinking rapidly, as if to regain my vision,

I wiped the back of my left hand over my eyes. As I did so, another sound defiled the silence. "Shhhrruuukkkkk!"

And, then I heard him.

"Skarl!"

My heart jumped in newfound hope! As my sight slowly returned, I beheld a great vision: the bench was moved away from the wall, and behind it was a small trap door just large enough for a person to squeeze through. How had I missed this door? With Lacina asleep on the bench, I'd not paid it as much attention as I should have, for fear of waking her.

Thankfully, though, it existed and protruding from this newfound door was the face of Jorgen!

"Come my friends! Quickly before the vile bastards return!"

Wasting no time, Lacina and I shimmied through the trapdoor. Once inside we found ourselves in a crawl space barely large enough for us to move about in. Jorgen handed me the torch, then moved past Lacina and myself and pulled the bench and trap door shut behind us. He then turned back to lead us further through the crawlspace.

"This way!" Jorgen urged. "If we move fast enough, we can make the shoreline before they know you're gone! But we must remain quiet, so our voices don't alert them."

Having to crawl for what seemed like hours, I finally spied a growing light in front of Jorgen. He too, noted the end of the darkness and said as much. "The morning light is just ahead, my friends. Almost there!" Knowing the dawn was near, I gauged we'd been imprisoned for roughly ten hours – and marveled at how the darkness had played such tricks with my ability to decipher the passing of time.

Within a few more minutes, we were climbing out of the crawlspace and into a small clearing in the woods. I helped Lacina out of the space, before looking around to ascertain our whereabouts. Through the black trees, I could barely make out the river's edge in the distance.

"The boat is down shore a little further," Jorgen asserted. "I didn't want to leave it too close for fear of discovery."

"How did you know of this means of escape, Jorgen?" my curiosity finally rose up.

"I told you, Skarl, my master was of the artisan's guild," Jorgen relied. "The first time we journeyed to the old fort, he shared the escape tunnel's location with his son. I think he merely believed his boy would find it fascinating. As the story went, the tunnel was dug by the first Ysling chieftain as a means of escape should the fort ever be overrun. The cell you were in, at the back of the black maze, all were meant to slow down any pursuit, allowing him time to flee through the crawlspace as his pursuers wandered aimlessly through the twisting, turning hallways that lead hither and yon."

The thought of battle and pursuit brought my hand involuntarily down to grab my axe – only to grip the empty air. The Yslings not only had my axe, but Lukas' rune sword. While getting Lacina to safety was of the utmost importance to me, I could not simply leave the weapons behind. My mind raced through options of how best to secret Lacina somewhere safe, perhaps the *Down Below*, before returning for the weapons. I was just about to voice this plan to Jorgen and Lacina when yet another surprise interrupted our journey.

CHAPTER TWENTY ONE: *TRISTAN!*

"Clever as always, I see!" Tristan's voice cut through the morning air like a poisoned knife. Standing on the shore, blocking us from Jorgen's boat, stood the traitor and a dozen Ysling warriors. He glowered at us, not trying to conceal his hatred for me in the slightest. And why should he? His father, my father, the seer – none were here to cast judgement on him for his treachery. No, it was clear Tristan felt empowered by his betrayal, his new alliance, his new… 'friends'.

"When Viggo told me of the tunnel from the cell, I figured it only a matter of time before you discovered it's whereabouts," the traitor grated with contempt. "Thank you for not making me wait much longer, tis terribly boring standing around with nothing to do other than anticipating your death, Skarl."

As he spit my name out, he pulled my axe from behind him with his right hand and aimed it menacingly in my direction. A quick glance showed the rune sword hung upon his opposite hip. Finally, after a lifetime of impotence, Tristan held all the cards.

"Tis a shame that I'll have to kill the lovely Lacina as well," he continued. "But, honestly the toughest part of the decision to slit her throat is which one of you will I force to watch the other die?"

Unable to control myself, I reflexively took a step towards Tristan as he waved the axe in Lacina's direction. As one the Ysling warriors drew their swords and single bladed axes, as they prepared to strike me down before I could close the gap between Tristan and myself.

"Oh, look at the mighty Skarl Kirwall, ever ready for battle as always," he sneered. "Oh, how I've longed to take this axe and wipe your stain from this life, Skarl. I've hated you for longer than I can remember. Always the favored, always the winner, always the one showered in praise," he paused for a moment as his eyes moved from me to Lacina. "Always the one to get the girl…

"Now, do us all a favor and get on your knees," he motioned to the ground in front of me with the axe. "We have work to do and, once again, you're in my way."

I stared into his eyes with a ferocity reserved for enemy combatants. Not only had I no intention of complying with his order, but I certainly had no desire to throw down my life while he still drew breath.

Realizing I was not going to give him the satisfaction, Tristan motioned to the Yslings closest to me. "Put him on his knees!" he roared with the same sort of immature rage I'd seen throughout our lives – as if his anger could someone allow him to get his way, remold reality in a manner that suited his dark heart.

From each side, a warrior moved towards us. With Lacina between us, Jorgen to the right and myself on the left, the warrior closer to Jorgen would have to move past him to get to me. Seeing my opening, my right hand shot in front of Lacina and shoved Jorgen bodily into the Ysling on his side. In a blur of motion, I came back the other way, just in time to catch the other warriors descending sword stroke. I blocked his arm with my left hand and spun into him, bringing my elbow up and around to crash into the side of his head while my right hand took the sword from his grasp. My motion continued in another arc that saw the length of his own steel rip upward into his gut, killing him instantly.

"Kill them!" Tristan yelled as he back pedaled towards the water – all signs of his recent façade of bravado gone.

I glanced toward Jorgen and saw he had similar success with the warrior I'd shoved him into, disarming and subsequently killing the man before the others could react. Lacina stepped back, and was eyeing the coming battle, clearly looking for a way to enter the fray. All this information came to me in a split second before I ducked to miss a death stroke swung at me by another Ysling. The force of his swing pulled him off balance just enough to allow me to slip past his guard and slash his throat with the tip of my stolen blade.

Before his body hit the ground two more were upon me, seeking to drive me back. Kicking out with my left leg, I knocked one back into the warriors behind him, bowling several of them over. The other managed to slash my right arm with his sword, before I could bring my hilt around to strike him a hard blow to the side of the head. He stumbled to my right, clearly knocked senseless by the impact. At once, a silken blur stepped in, pulled the long knife from his belt and plunged it into his chest over and over before he fell to the ground, dead. Wasting not a second, Lacina grabbed his sword and joined Jorgen who was fighting off two other Ysling warriors.

Seeing my opening, I leapt over the downed warriors between myself and Tristan, my sword arcing downward in a double fisted swing aimed at his forehead. He raised the axe to block the blow, but his lack of commitment to training, to strengthening himself, to heeding the warrior knowledge imparted to us by my father, Kjell Helvig and Einer Jor'Heim nearly proved fatal in that instant.

As my swing came down into the steel sheathed haft of the axe, Tristan's grip proved inadequate allowing the force of my blow to knock the weapon from his hands. When he realized he'd lost his grip, he backpedaled quickly, scurrying to draw Lukas' rune sword from his belt.

Transferring the sword from my right hand to the left, I reached down into the sand, and grabbed Father's axe, *my axe*, from where the traitor had dropped it. As my fingers closed on the haft, the voices of my ancestors roared in my thoughts.

"BEHIND YOU!"

Wheeling about, I brought the axe up just in time to ward off an Ysling swing meant to decapitate me. Driving his blade to my right, I brought the Ysling sword I still clutched in my left hand upward, into his chest where it stuck. Using the momentum from the blow, I pushed him over into a heap of dead bodies.

Quickly taking stock, I noted Jorgen and Lacina had made quick work of all but two remaining Yslings. Within a few seconds they joined their brethren in whatever Hel Yslings journeyed to when they died.

Knowing Tristan still remained, I turned back towards the traitor, who was walking slowly backwards towards the river. He held the rune sword out, prepared to see what damage he might do before his life slipped through his fingers.

I moved toward him as a snow lion might approach wounded prey. My eyes scanned his stance, the ground around him, the river behind, and I slowly closed the gap between us. Like a cornered animal, his head moved from side to side, trying desperately to spy some sort of escape, but there was none to be found.

It was then he did the unexpected. Glancing down quickly at the rune sword, he lifted his eyes back to mine, then spun around and hurled the blade as far as he could out into the river. To his credit, it was a mighty throw that saw the sword sail nearly the length of our Great House before splashing into the waters and sinking into the depths.

Puzzled by this action, my expression betrayed my thoughts as Tristan turned back to me.

"No Skarl, not only shall you not possess two legendary weapons, you'll also not enjoy the glory of killing me in a fair fight," he hissed. He smiled in a manner I'd grown accustomed to seeing whenever he'd successfully cheated someone in our youth. "There is no honor in killing an unarmed opponent for you or any other Kirwall warrior and you know this all too well."

He was right, there was no honor in killing a defenseless opponent, no matter how descpicable he was. And, by our laws, one such as that would have to be taken into custody to stand trial before the entire clan, at which point his fate would be decided. Knowing Tristan, he hoped for the opportunity to escape long before such a trial could convene, especially with the only living Kirwall's standing on that beach at that very moment.

Despite his newest ruse, I was unrestrained by his words or actions and continued moving closer to him, the lust to see his blood spilled still coursing through my veins – while I was the Runemaster, the executor of Justice, cold blooded murder was never just. While it seemed I wrestled with this for many moments, I'm sure it was but a few seconds.

As I drew near enough to close the gap between Tristan and myself in one quick step, I noticed Tristan's gaze break from mine and look off to my right. The look of cunning confidence on his face splintered into an expression of sudden terror.

In one move, faster than I could react, Lacina was past me, long knife in hand jammed into Tristan's throat. While I could not see the look upon her face, her tightened shoulders and almost trembling arms and legs spoke a tale of barely restrained rage.

"Not this time, Tristan," Lacina growled at him. "You forget the shield maiden's code of honor. If any man attempts to defile one of us, there is great glory in his death at our hands. And, while you may have been able to hide behind your father the last time you tried to force yourself on me when I was still in training, I'm a full shield maiden now."

"B-but —" before he could finish his final sentence, Lacina angrily jerked the long knife to her right, slicing his throat open so deeply, the blade nearly struck his spine. She reflexively pushed him away as Tristan tried to grasp her, before falling to his knees. He reached up in a vain attempt to stay the flow of blood from the wound, but it poured through his fingers faster than he could hope to stop it.

With a final, pathetic whining noise, Tristan Angivar, son of Kirwall Chieftain Sigurd Angivar, betrayer of his people, traitor to our clan, fell forward into the sand and died.

+++

The next day, we were once more in the large cave of the *Down Below*. The atmosphere was joyous and full of celebration, unlike the last time I'd been there. Osherah lied above in smoking ruins, the Ysling people were decimated and scattered. Even better, with minimal loss of life all the slaves had been freed.

Most importantly to me was what captivated my gaze, in front of me, my beautiful Lacina laughed as she conversed happily with Darla, the mother of Edrho and mastermind behind this underground town that had previously led to the escape of countless Ysling slaves and ultimately to the release of them all in the last few days. For the first time in several moons, I was finally content. While the loss of my parents, our clan, Runolf and Edrho weighed heavy on my heart, knowing we had avenged them and Lacina was still walking this life with me gave me great solace. There would be time enough in eternity to see my friends and family once more.

"And what will you do now?" I heard Lacina ask Darla.

"I must admit there's a part of me that wishes to cling to these caverns, stay here and live out the rest of my days," Darla replied wistfully. "But, Viggo still lives and it's only a matter of time before he pulls his forces back together and works to rebuild Osherah. While it will take him years to undo the damage we've wrought on this forsaken place, his evil will continue to stain the very ground around us.

"Perhaps I'll sail south with Jorgen. Return to my people, or even travel to his lands. Who knows, right now I prefer to live in the moment, bask in the glory that the Three Fates have seen fit to fulfill my desire to bring freedom to all those enslaved by Viggo and his ilk.

"What about you, child?" Darla turned the question back on Lacina. "Whither will you and young Skarl go?"

Lacina's eyes fell to the floor for an instant, before she turned and looked right at me with a knowing smile. We exchanged a glance that shared more than words before she replied. "We are going to meet our destiny."

EPILOGUE

ammers banged, swords clashed, budding warriors yelled and work
crews sang. Several seasons had passed since that fateful morning in
Osherah and while we would never forget our time there, the Ysling town
was just a memory now, for all of us.

It was good to see our village bustling with new life, new activity. So
far, we'd managed to rebuild all but a handful of the long houses and today
we were about to complete the Great House my family had lived in. While
the efforts had not been easy, we felt a surge of pride with each successive
victory in the rebuilding process. Kirwall was no longer a burned husk of
a village filled with memories of the dead, but a vibrant new home for so
many who had no other place to call their own.

Before quitting the shores of the Isle of Azekah and leaving the scorched
ruins of Osherah behind us, Lacina had cast the vision of a new Kirwall
to Darla, Jorgen and the rest of the freed slaves. This new village would be
home to anyone among us who cared to go. And, going forward any weary
traveler who sought shelter and peace would be welcome at our hearth.

Darla and the others had discussed it for a short time before coming
to full agreement: we would sail for the Bay of Abiathar as soon as possible. It took a bit to gather enough boats to bring us all back across the
Sea of Ashgul, but the gods were with us in this new endeavor. The unsea-
sonably calm seas of our voyage was enough to convince me that Adon
himself smiled upon us. Within a few weeks of our arrival, we'd buried my
dead clansmen, including my Father and mother, cleared away the debris
and begun reconstructing Kirwall for her new citizens. While the Yslings
had taken what valuables they could find, they failed to take what really
mattered: the tools we needed to rebuild. And more importantly, they left
behind the Kirwall spirit.

Everywhere I looked freed slaves from more cultures and backgrounds
than I'd ever known existed were working to build a new life in our new
home. After some discussion, we'd named Jorgen Chieftain. His first act
was to name Darla his advisor and right hand. Together, we worked out a
plan for rebuilding, assigned homes to all the former slaves who were now
free citizens, begun reconstruction and, lastly, I'd started training all the
able-bodied men to fight. No matter how idyllic our new way of life was,
the wolves still howled in the distance and the threat of a raid or worse, all
out invasion, lingered still.

Not to be outdone, Lacina had taken on the task of raising up new shield maidens. While many of the young women came from cultures where only the men fought, several took to the sword as if they were born of it. Pride welled within my breast as I watched my love pour all she had into their training, just as Skadiya had done with Lacina and her now dead peers.

WHACK!

The flat of Lacina's sword caught the fleshy part of a shield maiden-to-be's backside. The girl was roughly seventeen winters old but had a ferocity in her eyes that reminded me of Lacina at that age. She was slender, possessed of thick, dark curls that bounced when she moved and her skin had the same bluish tint Jorgen's possessed. She also had the same passion for victory Lacina stoked inside.

Grinding her jaw, the girl spun around and swung wildly in a fiery bid to strike her instructor. With a simple side-step, Lacina dodged the blow while reaching out with her left hand, grabbing the girl's shoulder and yanking her off balance in the same manner Father had taught us to do so long ago.

"Remember Thyra," Lacina's voice carried on the sort of commanding tone one would expect from the wife of a Runemaster. "The moment you stop thinking in a fight is the moment you die." To further punctuate her point, the tip of Lacina's sword was now under the downed girl's chin, lifting it up so the two saw each other face to face. She went on to expand the thought, "Many believe fighting is all about reflexes, muscle memory, the ability to react without thought. But not thinking is what leads a warrior to their death. No, you must already know what to anticipate, what moves are at your disposal at every counter and think with such speed that it appears to be simple, instinctive reaction."

Pulling her sword back, Lacina sheathed it before reaching down to help Thyra up from the ground. "That's enough for today. Go. Wash up for supper, for tonight we dine in the Great House!"

The shield maidens in training voiced a variety of positive expressions at this announcement before moving back towards the long houses, where hot baths and clean clothes awaited them.

At this, I turned back to the male warriors I was putting through a parry and counter-strike exercise. Spotting two fellows who were struggling, I leapt between them with my sword, kicked one's legs out from under him before spinning around and striking the other man in the shoulder, knocking him from his feet as well. Both fell into a heap on the ground, easy prey for one still standing above them.

"You must always be aware of everything around you in a fight, men!"

I bellowed loud enough for all to hear. "If you become so focused on your opponent that you lose your surroundings, death will surely come for you unawares. In fact, even in single combat you must use your surroundings to your advantage. Perhaps backing your opponent into an obstacle or forcing them into a position that hinders their movement. While it's always good to have exacting focus on your enemy, learn to develop your peripheral vision as well so you can use the world around you as a weapon."

"Now, go, wash up and we'll see you in the Great House this evening!"

+++

Boisterous laughter filled the air as all about the room people ate, drank, told jokes and enjoyed each other's company. At the main table, Lacina sat to my left and Jorgen to my right. On Jorgen's other side sat the new object of his affections, Stara. She was the older sister of Thyra, the young shield maiden in training and the two shared many physical similarities, including the long, curly brown locks, piercing eyes and pronounced cheekbones common to the culture Jorgen came from. She was nearly as intelligent as Lacina, quick witted and kept Jorgen in check, bringing out the best in him in all circumstances. They would make a fine family, of that I had no doubt.

All about the hall we saw new families emerging, slaves from all cultures and creeds finding love and hope for a future with one another. Twas strange to see this mixture of people celebrating in the Great House, but somehow, it just felt right.

My beautiful Lacina, dressed in a flowing, blue silk gown with snow lion heads embroidered onto each shoulder, stood up and raised her drinking horn aloft, as if in answer to my thoughts. "To Jorgen and Stara!" she spoke loudly so as to cut through the revelry. "May their marriage be full of love, grace, richness and..." she paused and looked conspiratorially at Stara, before continuing. "Many, *many* children!"

The people erupted in cheers as one. Several men jeered at Jorgen in a teasing manner that elicited no end of laughter. As their voices died down, Lacina toasted.

"Skol!"

As one the people responded, "SKOL!!"

Unable to contain himself, Jorgen turned to Stara and blurted out the question foremost on his mind, "Are you with child?"

Stara looked up into his eyes, small tears of joy welling up from her bottom eyelids as a rich smile played across her lips. She began nodding emphatically before answering. "I am, Jorgen, with your child. The Three Fates have shown me it's a boy."

Overcome with joy, Jorgen stood up, pulled Stara to her feet and embraced her. Then, he too, raised his drinking horn to the crowd and yelled, "A toast! To the most amazing woman I have ever met! Long live Stara, and long live our children!"

Once again, the crowd roared back, "SKOL!!"

As the night wore on, we laughed, loved, drank and enjoyed one another's company through games, challenges and tales of amazing stories. It was truly a night for the ages. But, one that would find itself rudely interrupted.

The doors flew open and in came a young man, scarcely fifteen winters old. I recognized him as Jakob, the newest member of our warriors, tasked with sentry duty guarding over the newly rebuilt Kirwall village.

"My lords!" Jakob yelled out loud enough to quiet the room. "My lords! Come quickly!"

Standing to my feet, my right hand involuntarily went to the haft of my axe, resting upon my belt. "What is it, Jakob? What disturbs your peace on such a night as this?"

"Riders my lord! Many armed riders approaching from the south..." his voice trailed off for a second as he caught his breath. "And, they don't appear to be coming in peace!"

"To sword and axe!" I yelled, effectively ending the banquet we were enjoying only seconds before. As one we moved out of the Great House and into the square, weapons at the ready. Most of Kirwall was now populated by freed slaves. And, of them, only a handful had ever experienced real combat. While I knew Jorgen and Lacina were hardened warriors, the others who could make the same claim could be counted on one hand.

As the riders came into view over the crest of the hill. It was clear battle would soon be upon us. Knowing this, I raised Father's axe, *my* axe, to my lips and whispered an incantation...

THE END

ABOUT OUR CREATORS

WRITER –

MIKE BULLOCK —suffers greatly from a vicious malady: the highly combustible mixture of an overactive imagination and an intense case of thaasophobia (the unnatural fear of boredom). These two forces are constantly battling in his mind and the only treatment for this unnamed syndrome is to create something... anything. Whether it's painting an electric guitar, writing a song, dreaming up fantastical new worlds or crafting the novel you now hold in your hands. Thankfully, there is a way you can help! Read this book, then have a friend read it, then another and another. While Mike's beautiful wife, Angie, might counter this with a well-placed remark like, "Please don't encourage him..." it's really the only way to relieve his suffering. Thank you for making a difference in the life of this author and his poor wife and son who have to put up with him.

INTERIOR ILLUSTRATOR –

CHRIS NYE —has been a graphic artist and illustrator for over 30 years. He has actively worked in the comic book and graphic novel industry since 2001. In addition to work for Airship 27 Productions, he is currently working on comic book projects for Sitcomics and Markosia. He is also a graphic artist, illustrator and writer with Lockheed Martin. He resides in Simpsonville, South Carolina.

COVER ARTIST –

STEVE OTIS – started to draw at a very early age. Fueled by images of DC and Marvel comics. He soon discovered the great Warren magazines (Creepy and Eerie in the early 70's). From there he began to delve more deeply into horror, gothic and sci fi type art. Heavily influenced by Frazetta, Boris and Richard Corben, he began experimenting in oil paints in 1988.

His first desire was to become a fantasy illustrator and did quite a bit of work in that style in the late 90's for CCG (collectible card games). By the early 2000's he started using exclusively acrylics. He began to look for techniques to challenge his artistic style in a more "Fine Art" vein while keeping a firm thematic of dark art.

He taught art in high school for 10 years before concentrating on painting. He has produced quality work as a comic artist, illustrator, sculptor. Active as an artist since 1990 Steve began focusing his efforts in the world in fine (dark) art in 2005. Since then he has participated in many solo exhibitions and collective art shows in Quebec, Montreal, Italy and a few states in the USA.

All for One

COMING SOON!

From the pages of Alexandre Dumas' classic adventure novels come the Three Musketeers. The King of France's personal guard will pledge their loyalty to their country and themselves in their boisterous cry, "All for one and one for all!" Now these colorful characters are back. First we have Athos, the veteran soldier who lives with a broken heart. Then we have Aramis, the priest turned swordsman. Finally there is Porthos, the larger than life rascal with a giant appetite for food, women and adventure. All of them watching over their young protégé, the handsome and daring D'Artagnan.

In two fast-paced action tales and one thrill-packed novella, these four famous heroes are back to thrill and excite new readers. From Italy, to Spain and then the new world of Canada, these men will take on any and all villainy as only they can. New Pulp scribes Joel Jenkins, Paul Beale and Alan J. Porter deliver three amazing tales continuing the exploits of Dumas' cavalier musketeers.